5 Reasons why you will love this book

A brilliant fantasy adventure series.

Perfect for fans of Fantastic Beasts and Where to Find Them film.

The Companions are a secret society protecting mythical creatures living amongst us.

A page-turner to keep you on the edge of your seat!

From brilliant author, Julia Golding.

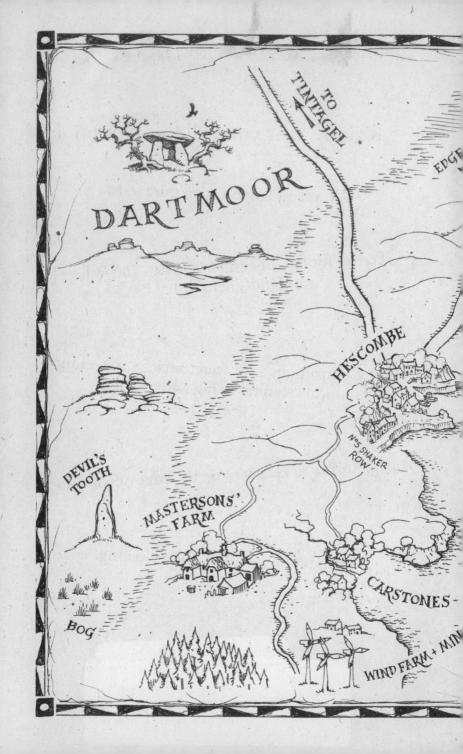

MOOR
AL PARK

CHARTMOUTH

REFINERY

MILSOM St.

MALLINS
WOOD

COASTAL PATH

THE STACKS

HESCOMBE
CHANNEL

OXFORD
UNIVERSITY PRESS

Great Clarendon Street, Oxford OX2 6DP

Oxford University Press is a department of the University of Oxford. It furthers the University's objective of excellence in research, scholarship, and education by publishing worldwide. Oxford is a registered trade mark of Oxford University Press in the UK and in certain other countries

First published 2007
First published in this paperback edition 2018

Data available

ISBN: 978-0-19-276666-3

1 3 5 7 9 10 8 6 4 2

Printed in Great Britain

Paper used in the production of this book is a natural, recyclable product made from wood grown in sustainable forests. The manufacturing process conforms to the environmental regulations of the country of origin.

Julia GOLDING

Mines of the Minotaur

OXFORD
UNIVERSITY PRESS

Contents

1

White Horses

The front door of Number Five Shaker Row clicked open. A girl in a white nightdress walked steadily down the path, bare feet not flinching from the freezing paving stones. Pushing the gate wide, she crossed the lane to the steps leading to the beach. The tide was in, lapping at the pebbles at the high water mark. The moon hung in the sky like a circle of ice. A gentle breeze lifted long black strands of hair, teasingly wrapping them over her face.

She flitted down the steps and crunched across the pebbles, ignoring the cut made in her heel by a shard of glass. Moving swiftly, she came to the water's edge. Sea-foam caressed her toes as waves slapped on shore.

She paused, absorbing the calm around her.

Then, raising her arms above her head, the girl opened her mouth, clenched her fists, and gave out a deep, rumbling roar—a sound out of all proportion to her size. It poured from her like the onset of an avalanche, echoing across the sea. The elements were alert to her call. Wave crests formed out in the channel; the wind began to pick up strength; clouds straggled across the moon, blotting its face.

The girl's white nightdress now flapped against her legs. Her hair twisted and writhed in the spray whipped from the sea. A lid lifted off the rubbish bin of Number Four and rolled down the street on its rim in a crazy wobble. A door banged.

Opening her fists, pointing her fingers at the sky, the girl called down the storm's power. A forked lightning bolt leapt from a cloud to touch the tip of her index finger, illuminating her in a halo of crackling white light. A deafening boom of thunder rolled across the skies. Rain fell in torrents, plastering the girl's hair against her scalp. Waves crashed about her knees, trying to pull her down, but she stood firm. The largest surges clawed at the cliff behind, working to undermine the rock.

The storm-raiser laughed.

Pleased with the fury of the onslaught, she sent the tempest inland, directing it with a jerk of an arm over her head.

Unleashed upon the streets of Hescombe, the storm wound among the houses like a crowd of rampaging hooligans, up-ending bins, blowing loose tiles from roofs, uprooting trees to fall on walls and cars, crushing them like cardboard. Car alarms wailed. A ginger cat streaked across the empty roads, seeking shelter from the hail of missiles.

On the beach, waves crashed against the cliffs as the wind howled like a wolf. Spray flung itself into the air to dash on the pebbles at the girl's feet. Out to sea, as the breakers rolled inland, shapes appeared on the crests of the waves. Storm-tossed manes and flying hooves galloped headlong towards her, whinnying in tormented voices. Reaching the shore, the white horses of the sea converged on the girl. They danced around her, leaping, their legs arched. Foam flew as they smashed into each other in the stampede. They had not been released from their stables for many long years and rejoiced to find a new companion. She, however, was oblivious to them, wrapped up in the storm she had summoned. Spurred on to test their bond, one stallion split from the herd and cantered along the edge of a breaker. It collided with the girl, dousing her with water as it dispersed in a flurry of spray. Jolted from her tempest-dream by this fleeting encounter, she gasped for breath, let her arms fall, and crumpled to her knees. With equal suddenness the storm dropped, the waves subsided, and the remaining horses faded into shapeless foam, tossed like a white mane at the sea's margin.

Now the storm had passed, Col Clamworthy and Skylark, his pegasus companion, emerged from their shelter to trot home along the beach. Forced to land, they had taken refuge in a sea-cave while the tempest blew itself out. They were now enjoying the return to peace in a comfortable silence, Col's fingers wrapped in Skylark's snowy mane. Col loved these times with Skylark—they were what he lived for—but he knew they soon had to part.

The little port of Hescombe was just round the next headland and the pegasus must not be seen by other humans.

'Ready to fly again?' Col asked.

Skylark sniffed the air. 'Yes, the storm's gone. It should be safe for me now.'

'You'd better get going then.' Col yawned: it must be four in the morning.

Skylark shook his mane, trying to stay awake. 'Trust a party organized by your father to be such a riot. My head aches from all that rock-dwarf music.'

'So does mine.' Col leant against Skylark's neck, breathing in the familiar smells of hay and horse. 'Thanks for coming.' He slid from Skylark's back to the ground.

'My pleasure. It was worth it just to see your father with the Kraken,' replied the pegasus with a whinnying laugh.

'Yeah.' Col grinned. 'That was cool.'

Col still hadn't recovered from his father's abrupt announcement the week before that he had decided to marry again. He was perhaps even more shocked that Evelyn Lionheart, a friend of Mack's since childhood, had said 'yes'—she had no excuse of ignorance and must know exactly what she was taking on.

'You know, Skylark, my dad has a definite wild streak,' Col mused. 'Just look at the party tonight.'

'Yes—it's not often that the host abandons his guests like that,' said Skylark.

Col's father had celebrated his engagement with a beach barbecue for his friends in the Society for the

Protection of Mythical Creatures. The evening must have felt too tame for him because, at midnight, he had on impulse run into the sea clad only in his boxer shorts. He had dived under the surface, emerging a few seconds later spouting seawater in a glistening arc. Then out of the water had emerged one of the long tentacles of the Kraken. The limb had curled around the swimmer and lifted him high into the air, Mack shouting with delight as he soared upwards. With a snap of its tentacle, the Kraken had cast him out to sea. Mack had disappeared under the water but soon popped up again, shaking droplets from his hair.

Col had been impressed but also frightened. He had never seen his father on the surface with the Kraken before: it was quite something. The Kraken challenged the skill of his companion with five more throws, each one calling for more difficult and extravagant dives from Mack. The competition over, apparently to the satisfaction of both, Mack had swum back, accepting the applause of the onlookers as his due. Mack thrived on the primitive challenge of man against beast—the danger excited him. He would have had no sympathy had he known his son's fears on his behalf.

'That party was my dad all over,' Col told Skylark. 'I just hope Evelyn knows what she's doing.'

Skylark snorted sceptically.

'I wonder what Connie thinks of her aunt marrying him.' Col hadn't yet come to terms with the prospect of his father abandoning his life on the road and moving in to Shaker Row, only a few streets from where Col lived with his grandmother. It felt really weird that he and his best friend, Connie, would now in some ways be 'sharing' his dad. He felt a little jealous of her as there was no talk of him being invited into the household after the marriage.

'Yes, it's going to be hard for everyone,' Skylark agreed, reading his companion's conflicting feelings through the bond between them. 'A Kraken, a banshee, and a universal companion under one roof: perhaps you're better off with your gran?'

Col laughed softly. 'Thanks, Skylark. See you later.'

The pegasus galloped down the strand, white wings beating for take off. Once airborne, Skylark disappeared over the cliffs in the direction of Dartmoor. Col turned and began to trudge home, hands shoved deep in his pockets.

Col would never have noticed Connie if he hadn't almost tripped over her. She was curled in a ball on the stretch of beach in front of her aunt's house, asleep. He looked up and down the shore: it was deserted. What was she doing here?

'Connie?' Col shook her gently by the shoulder.

Her eyes flickered open for a second, then closed.

'Connie? Are you all right?' Col was concerned now—this wasn't like her at all. 'What's happened?'

Connie's eyes opened again and this time she uncurled. She rubbed her arm across her face.

'Where am I?'

A wave broke on the pebbles a few metres away, pawing at the stones like restless hooves.

Col touched her arm. She was freezing, soaked to the skin. 'We'd better get you indoors.'

Connie scrambled up stiffly. Clutching her wet nightdress to her body, she saw that the arm and leg on which she had been lying were deeply marked by the imprint of the stones. She must have been here for some time. A whisper of memory returning, she suddenly felt scared—scared of what she had done. She moved a step away from Col, gazing at him as if he were a stranger.

Unnerved, Col tried to make light of it. 'You probably walked in your sleep.'

She shook her head, her whole body shivering. 'I d-don't sleepwalk.'

'Come on: let me help you back.' He held out his hand.

'I'll manage.' Wincing with pain, Connie stumbled up the beach unaided as fast as she could. She hobbled to the back door of Number Five and found the spare key under the flowerpot.

Col knew he couldn't leave her like this. He followed her in. The house was quiet—Evelyn sound asleep upstairs. A clock ticked in the hall. Connie limped through the kitchen and into the front room where there was an old electric fire. She switched it on and sank on to the sofa, wrapping herself in a blanket. Col stood in the doorway, watching her.

'What's going on, Connie? You do know, don't you?'

'I . . . I'm not sure.' Connie felt humiliated that Col was seeing her like this; she wished he would go.

'I'll make you some tea.'

He went into the kitchen, leaving her alone in front of the fire. Her skin smarted in the heat, red-raw as if it had been flayed by a whip. Feeling down to check her numb toes, she discovered that her heel was bleeding. When had she cut herself?

The clock continued to tick calmly in the hall, out of step with the stormy sea of panic surging inside her. She could make no sense of this. How had she ended up on the beach? She felt a hum in her bones as if she had been encountering some powerful creature. As the single living universal companion in the Society for the Protection of Mythical Creatures, Connie was the only person able to communicate with all creatures. That meant she could have been bonding with anything. But what beast or being had the power to draw her out of her house without her knowing about it? And what had they done together?

Her suspicions turned to Kullervo, the shape-shifting creature who was her enemy—and her companion. He was her counterpart in the mythical world, able to assume any shape and communicate with all creatures. She had encountered him twice over the past two years and each time only barely escaped with her life. In a desire to punish mankind for the damage they had done to the world, Kullervo intended to destroy humanity. To do this, he needed the universal to channel his formidable powers so he could wipe people from the face of the earth.

Had he been here tonight?

Connie bit her lip, hardly daring to feel out for his presence as she knew she should. Surely he wasn't? The Society said he was in the Far East. Six of the leaders, known as the Trustees, had gone to fight him and his weather giants in that region. He couldn't be in two places at once—could he?

Long shivering minutes dragged past. Exhaustion gained the upper hand; the warmth of the fire caught her like a tide and began to drag her into sleep. The photos on the mantelpiece swum before her eyes; the figurine of the bronze bear gleamed softly; the statue of a white marble horse leaping from the waves shone with a frosty light. Connie drifted into a state of half-sleep. Images flickered in her mind: the flash of lightning, white horses arching over her, pale hands raised to a black sky. Hands—her hands!

Connie woke with a start from her drowse and stared down at her palms, turning them over, searching for a sign of what had happened to them. They seemed exactly the same as usual—if a little blue with cold around the nails. Yet she knew that they had done something bad.

But what?

Col returned with two mugs of tea and sat beside her, nursing his in his palms, waiting for her to speak.

'I think I summoned a storm.' The confession tumbled out. She hadn't meant to say anything, but Col was her closest friend, and he was here—it was difficult to keep it from him.

'You what?' Col put his mug down. He felt angry, remembering how spooked Skylark had been as the wind had blown him about. 'You mean you did that? But Skylark and I were out in it—we had to land—didn't you think of the damage you might be doing? Why on earth did you do it?'

'I . . . I don't know.'

'What was it? Weather giant?'

Connie gave a miserable shrug.

Col stared at her: her mismatched green-brown eyes, so like his own odd pair, seemed very large and scared. He'd not seen her so unsure of herself for a long time. Whatever had happened, she clearly hadn't done it on purpose. His mood softened into anxious pity for her. 'You've got to tell someone,' he said.

She gave a hiccup of laughter. 'I'm telling you.'

'No, I mean someone who can help— Evelyn . . .?'

She looked down. 'I can't bother her—she's all excited about the wedding.'

'Don't be stupid—she'd want to know.'

Connie clenched her fists in her lap. 'No, I'm not spoiling everything for her. I'll . . . I'll sort it out. Maybe it was just . . . just something that happens to universals. I mean, none of us know how . . . how . . .'

She stopped. Col felt she had pushed him away by bringing up her gift. Of course he didn't know what it was like to be her—he was only a pegasus companion. Connie was unique—and part of him was frightened of her powers. He didn't fool himself that he was any match for her.

'OK, fine,' he said stiffly. 'I'd better go.'

Connie realized she'd upset him. 'I'm sorry, Col, I didn't mean it to sound like that.'

'Yeah, I know.' Feeling he had been too quick to take offence, he gave her a proper smile. 'Look, why don't you sleep on it? I will as well. We can think what to do when we're not like a pair of zombies.'

'OK. But you won't say anything to anyone, will you?' Connie felt desperate to keep her role in creating the storm secret; she was ashamed of her loss of self-control.

'I won't if you don't want me to, but—'

She interrupted him quickly. 'Thanks, Col. See you tomorrow then.'

He got up, wondering if he was doing the right thing leaving her without waking Evelyn. 'Yeah, it's Rat's assessment, don't forget to come early.' He picked up the mugs to take back to the kitchen.

'No, I won't.'

'Will you be OK now?'

'Yeah, I'll be fine.'

When he'd gone, Connie stayed where she was. She pressed her knuckles in her eyeballs and pummelled herself awake. White streaks swirled before her closed lids.

Not as white as the light that had pierced them earlier, a voice in her head whispered.

The clock in the hall struck six and Connie heard the central heating hum into life. A bath: that was what she needed. A nice, warm bath that would wash away this nightmare.

But as the water pounded into the iron bathtub standing on its clawed feet, Connie heard an echo of the fury of the waves. She knew then that she would not dare to close her eyes again until she had no choice but to give in to sleep.

2

Assessment Sunday

The next day was Assessment Sunday, when new members of the Society found out if they had a gift with mythical creatures. Connie cycled down the lane to her Uncle Hugh's cottage in plenty of time for Rat's test. The little house was at the far end of the Masterson estate, handy for a cove where Connie's great-uncle liked to go fishing. It was also convenient for the Society to conduct its assessments away from prying eyes as few people ventured down the private road. Hugh was not party to this fact, not being a member of the Society: he just thought he'd found a quiet spot to spend his retirement. Connie had been asked to ensure he stayed indoors—something she hoped to achieve with the bribe of a newspaper.

She let herself in the back door. 'Hi, Uncle Hugh. I've brought you a *Telegraph*.'

Hugh was still finishing his breakfast. He beamed at his niece over the toast rack. 'Thank you, my dear.

That was very thoughtful of you. Fancy coming all the way out here just to give an old man a treat!' He poured Connie a mug of tea from a chipped blue and white pot. 'Here, you might like to see this.'

He passed her a postcard from his sister, Godiva, currently in Brazil.

Connie read it through. 'Sounds as if she's having fun.'

'Yes, my sister has finally found herself after all these years. Joined your lot in Rio and learning Portuguese, would you believe it?'

Thanks to Connie, Godiva had last year admitted that she was a companion to wood sprites after years of rejecting the Society and everything to do with it.

'That's great—I'm really pleased.'

'And so am I, even if you are all as nutty as fruit cakes. How's Evelyn, by the way?'

'Oh, you know: excited about the wedding.'

Hugh gave his great-niece a shrewd look, taking in the tired shadows under her eyes. 'And has she said anything about where she and Mack are going to live afterwards? You know you're always welcome here if they don't have room for you—though I suppose it's a bit too quiet for a youngster.'

'Thanks, Uncle Hugh. I'd like to come for the Christmas holidays as they'll be on their honeymoon. I dunno after that. Evelyn's said that she doesn't expect life to change much.'

'Doesn't she now!' Hugh chuckled.

There was a thump and a shout from next door. Connie grimaced at her uncle. 'So how are you getting on with the neighbours?'

Connie's friend Rat had arrived in the area as part of the Ecowarrior encampment in Mallins Wood. When Mr Masterson gave Rat's father a job for the lambing season, the family had moved out of their chilly bus and taken up residence in the cottage next door to Hugh. Their introduction had been a disaster: Wolf, the family pet Alsatian, had thrown himself at Hugh in a jealous rage when he had seen the old man hugging his great-niece. Connie was a big favourite with Wolf.

'Well, apart from his heavy metal music, her screams when Rat does something to annoy her, and the menagerie of squawking animals the boy keeps in the coal shed, they're the perfect neighbours.' Hugh caught Connie's eye and winked. 'Don't worry: they're not too bad really. I'm rather fond of the boy and Mrs Ratcliff's got a heart of gold. They always turn down the music when I ask. Had me over to tea several times lately. I think we're getting rather pally.'

'That's good. I wouldn't like to get on the wrong side of Mrs Ratcliff.'

'I'll let you into a secret,' said Hugh in a conspiratorial whisper, 'she scares the living daylights out of me too. Given a choice, I think I'd prefer to take on the Alsatian.'

Connie laughed and took her mug to the sink to wash up. Looking out of the window, past Mrs Ratcliff's washing flapping in the breeze, to the blue autumnal sky, she heard the growl of motorbikes approaching. It was time.

'Is it OK if I go for a walk?'

Hugh had settled himself behind the newspaper. 'What's that?'

'I want to go out.'

'Of course. But you're not to go into the old tin mines. Oh, and don't go anywhere near the cliff-edge: a great chunk fell away during that storm the other night and the rest looks a bit shaky to me.'

Connie had been trying not to think about that. She gripped the edge of the sink.

'Did you hear, Connie?'

'Yes. I won't go near the edge.'

He looked up. 'Off you go then. Mustn't waste a lovely day like today inside.'

As Connie left the kitchen, she heard the rumble of engines more clearly now, heading in her direction. She arrived outside the Ratcliff gate at the same time as the two bikes. Dismounting quickly from his father's Harley-Davidson, Col greeted her with a quizzical look. She shook her head slightly. Now was not the moment to talk.

Mack parked the bike and slapped her heartily on the back, making her stagger.

'Hugh tucked up safely with the paper?' he asked. Connie nodded.

Dr Brock, the leader of the local chapter of the Society, got off the second motorcycle and bent over to assist the passenger in the sidecar, removing a series of packages and cages to allow him space to clamber out. With considerable difficulty, the Society's assessor, Mr Coddrington, unfolded himself like a telescope from the cramped confines of the sidecar. His thin face creased in a frown.

Connie moved away: Mr Coddrington always gave her the creeps. He seemed wrong somehow; her instinct told her that he wasn't fully alive to the world like other members of the Society naturally were. She never ceased to wonder how he had passed his own assessment. But then, his gift for weather giants was real enough: maybe she just didn't understand him—or them?

'This it then?' Mr Coddrington asked as he looked disdainfully at the small row of cottages. 'Where is the assessment to take place?'

'As I explained,' Dr Brock said patiently, 'Rat's family are not members of the Society.'

'Rat? What kind of name is that?'

'His real name is Sean Ratcliff. Anyway, Ivor, I thought that we could use the cove down the track here: it's sheltered from curious eyes.'

'Hmm. I don't like doing assessments outside. You can get interference with the result. But I suppose it will have to do.' Mr Coddrington's eyes lighted upon Connie and he turned to her with a chilly smile. 'Ah, Miss Lionheart, delightful as always to see you!' He held out his hand and Connie reluctantly shook it. 'You in particular will have to stand well back: we cannot have our universal confusing the assessors, can we?'

He was right. The assessors—a raven, a white mouse, and a green lizard—were already moving restlessly in their cages; a faint hum was emanating from the black velvet bag which Connie knew to hold the crystal.

'Of course, I'll keep well out of the way,' she said.

'Well, let's get on with it then,' said Mr Coddrington in a brisk tone. 'It looks as if the weather is on the turn.' He looked at his watch. 'Give us ten minutes,' he told Mack, 'I should be ready for him by then.'

The party divided and Connie led Mr Coddrington and Dr Brock down to the sea.

'So, Miss Lionheart, what have you been getting up to recently?' Mr Coddrington asked, smoothing his lank brown hair across his brow in defiance of the wind that was doing its best to dishevel it. On the surface his question sounded innocent, but Connie could not help but suspect that he had some ulterior reason for asking. He always made a point of keeping himself well informed about the activities of Society members. Did he somehow know about her storm-raising?

'Er, not much,' she said. Nothing I'd tell you, she added to herself.

'I wish I could be so fortunate,' Mr Coddrington remarked. 'Desk piled high with work—people constantly ringing me up—it's quite a breath of fresh air to escape from the office to do assessments like this.'

'Oh, really?' Dr Brock asked politely. 'Are there lots of new candidates? That would be encouraging.'

Mr Coddrington sniffed. 'Not especially. But I've taken on a lot of Frederick Cony's admin for him now he's too ill to manage it—I'm keeping the Trustees' office ticking over.'

'That's very kind of you.' But Connie thought Dr Brock did not sound pleased to hear of Mr Coddrington's expanded role. 'How is Frederick, by the way?' Dr Brock asked.

17

'Not good,' said the assessor, shaking his head. 'Not good, I'm afraid.'

They reached the cove to find it deserted: a smooth crescent of sand lapped by gentle waves, and with no unwanted visitors. Over to the west there was a new pile of earth and rock at the bottom of the cliff.

'Good thing the storm passed so quickly the other night before it did any more damage,' said Dr Brock, gesturing to the landslide. 'Did you hear it, Connie?'

Connie looked up at him guiltily. If she was going to tell someone, Dr Brock would be a good choice. His blue eyes smiled at her behind his gold-rimmed glasses, inviting her confidence. But what would he think if he knew the truth? Would he be angry with her? Fear her?

'Er . . . no . . . I slept right through it.' The lie out in the open, Connie felt even worse. She wanted to unsay it—blurt out the truth—but Mr Coddrington was hovering at her shoulder. She couldn't say anything now.

'Lucky you,' Dr Brock said. 'I couldn't sleep a wink—roof came off the bakery next door—tiles smashing all over my front garden.'

'Oh, I'm sorry.'

Dr Brock patted her on the back. 'Why are you sorry? After all, it wasn't your fault.'

Mr Coddrington jumped down onto the sand. 'Wait up there, Miss Lionheart,' he called. 'That should be far enough away. You can watch from there.'

Trying to push her guilty thoughts aside, Connie waited while the assessor and Dr Brock arranged the

18

equipment on the points of the compass: raven to the east, lizard to the south, mouse to the west, and crystal to the north.

'I wasn't expecting to be allowed to watch,' she murmured to Dr Brock when he rejoined her, leaving the assessor pacing the sands, checking the distances between the compass points.

'Well, it's not against the rules, but generally Ivor does these things in private. I think he's showing off because you're here.'

'Hey, Connie!' a voice called behind her.

Connie turned to see Col and Mack escorting Rat down the path. Rat's sharp-featured face was beaming; his unkempt nut-brown hair blew messily about in the wind: he for one looked completely at ease with the proceedings, as if he thought it all one big joke. As well he might, Connie reminded herself, as he had not yet been initiated into the mysteries of the Society and did not understand what today's test would mean for him.

'Hi, Rat,' Connie called back. 'Ready then?'

'Yeah. Wish me luck!'

Rat clattered down the wooden steps and crunched over the sand to Mr Coddrington. As the pair stood close together, Connie could see that Mr Coddrington was giving Rat the same talk he had given her at her assessment. Rat seemed not to be paying much attention, too preoccupied by the creatures in the cages.

'What's your money on then, Francis?' Mack asked Dr Brock as he stretched out on the grass, chewing a strand. 'Sea Snake like us?'

'Sadly not, I think,' said Dr Brock.

'I hope he's another pegasus companion,' said Col. 'It'd be great having another one in our region.'

'Heaven preserve us,' muttered Dr Brock. 'The skies would not be safe for us poor dragon riders.'

Col laughed. 'What do you think, Connie?'

'I think I can guess—but it won't be pegasi, I'm afraid, Col.'

'Go on, tell us what it is.'

She shook her head. 'That'd spoil the surprise. All I'll say is that someone close to him has given me a hint.'

Rat was now standing in the centre of the circle of objects. Mr Coddrington had to show him how to hold his arms out straight with palms pointing down as he evidently had not listened to the instructions. Laughing out loud at the absurdity of what he was asked to do, Rat began to spin like a compass needle. Bird, lizard, and mouse: all were passed and all remained silent. Finally, Rat turned to the crystal. Up on the bank, Connie hugged her jacket close, sensing a sudden drop in temperature; a stillness settled on the scene as the wind died. Then the crystal began to glow and rattle. Rat dropped his hands in surprise. He hadn't been expecting this.

Mr Coddrington nodded and took a folder from his briefcase. He drew Rat aside and began to run through a sheet of questions with him.

'What's he doing?' Connie asked.

'It's the next stage, don't you remember?' Col said—then stopped. 'Oh, of course, you didn't get this far, did you? The idiot failed you. It's the creature assessment: he's running through all Rat's previous experience with animals to see which one points to his companion species.'

The four spectators watched as Mr Coddrington bent over his papers. Rat was now taking things seriously, answering without any sidelong glances at his friends. The assessor then shut his folder with a snap and swept up his equipment. He shoved the mouse cage and the bag into Rat's arms and led the way as they scrambled back up the beach.

'Well, that was all very straightforward,' Mr Coddrington announced as he reached the top of the stairs. 'No surprises there.' He cast a surreptitious look in Connie's direction and she knew that he—like her—was thinking back to two years ago when she had given him the biggest surprise of his career. 'He clearly falls in the Company of the Elementals. I'll leave his induction to your chapter, of course, but my assessment is that his gift is likely to be with the frost wolf.'

Rat, who had been listening to all this with a bemused expression while he waited at the bottom of the steps, latched onto this last phrase.

'Frost wolf. So where's my wolf then?'

Connie broke into a laugh, seeing the expectant look on his face. Col hurried forward and took the cage and bag from Rat and pulled him up onto the path.

'It doesn't quite work like that,' Col said quickly. 'You'd better let me explain.'

That evening, the new members of the Chartmouth Chapter of the Society were inducted at a brief ceremony at the beginning of the Annual General Meeting. Rat had to wait outside with the three other young people while old members took their seats in the Mastersons' barn. The room was already full, but latecomers were still trying to squeeze in. Col was among them, having lingered with Rat in the yard. He climbed over the hay-bales to reach Skylark who was waiting for him at the far end of the Company of Two and Four-Legged Beasts and Beings, close to the Elementals so they could be next to Rat when he finally took his seat. Col settled down beside the pegasus, then looked around him for his other friends. Connie was on her own by the door, looking down at her hands. He wondered if he should call her over, but she was studiously ignoring everyone. She had successfully avoided the subject of the storm all day, taking cover in the excitement of Rat's assessment. They had to talk.

'Right, can I have everyone's attention, please,' Dr Brock called again. 'We've a busy agenda tonight. But first, let us welcome our newest members.'

Dr Brock's companion, Argand, a red-scaled dragon, opened the door with a sweep of his tail, revealing the four young people waiting nervously outside. Silence fell. Rat gazed in amazement at the ranks of creatures before him—great boars, griffins, rock dwarves, winged horses, dragons—more than could be taken in with one glance. A chorus of phoenixes and firebirds began to sing as Argand blew a ring of fire—the gateway through which each new companion had to pass. This ancient custom was a test of courage, but no one had been known to stay outside with so many wonderful creatures to encounter. The room erupted into applause as each new member leapt through, Rat with typical bravado turning a cartwheel for extra effect. Then they split up to take their seats among each of the four companies. Rat ran to a place in the Elementals near Col, grinning with relief that he had survived that ordeal unsinged.

Col punched him on the knee. 'You did that much better than me, show off!'

Dr Brock stood up again. 'A heartfelt welcome to our new members—I look forward to meeting each one of you at the party at the end of the meeting. But now to business: the re-election of the committee. We have no changes to announce this year. I have offered to continue as Chair as no one else has volunteered; Argot remains Vice-chair; Evelyn Lionheart, Treasurer; Lavinia Clamworthy, Secretary. We're still looking for a volunteer from High Flyers to take on a post on the committee, but you've all been very hard to pin down.' Dr Brock looked over at the group ranged on the eastern side of the barn. A laugh rippled around the room: the winged creatures and their companions were notorious for their ability to evade responsibility.

Col didn't join in the laughter, not finding it very funny: he had noticed that many members of the Society were getting increasingly apathetic. It started in the headquarters in London with men like Mr Coddrington getting in the way of any new ideas with their rules and regulations. That left the same people, like his grandmother and Dr Brock, doing all the work, fighting the battles with headquarters while the rest came along as passengers. How was the Society going to face the threat of Kullervo if they were so weak?

Rat tapped him on the knee, interrupting his thoughts. 'You've got a dragon on the committee?'

'Yeah, of course we have.' Col had been in the Society so long he'd forgotten that the equal role played by the mythical creatures might seem strange to someone from outside.

'Now, let's have the report on how our youngsters are doing,' declared Dr Brock making way for the next speaker.

Col's grandmother, a fine looking woman in her seventies with curly white hair, stepped into the centre of the circle. She started to read from her report, running through the progress made by the young companions in each of the four companies. Reaching the pegasi riders, she raised her voice a notch and said:

'Our chapter has again won the gold medal at the inter-chapter games held this summer in Scotland. Skylark and Col Clamworthy came top in their age category.' Applause broke out. Col gave Rat a sheepish smile; Skylark tossed his mane smugly.

After a pause to let the noise die down, Mrs Clamworthy continued. 'And last but not least, our universal has continued her training, concentrating this year on a technique called the hauberk.' She halted and looked over to the door. 'Have I got that right, Connie?'

'Yes,' Connie said briefly, keeping her head down.

'Would you like to tell us what it is?' Mrs Clamworthy coaxed her.

Connie reluctantly stood up and said in a voice that barely carried to the listeners, 'The hauberk is a way for a universal to assume the protective powers of a mythical creature.' She stopped, twisting her fingers nervously together. She wished everyone would stop smiling at her, thinking she was so wonderful, when she knew she didn't deserve their approval.

'That sounds very interesting,' Dr Brock encouraged her. 'Can you give us an example to help us understand?'

Connie was still looking down. 'I've tried it with Argand, the golden dragon. When I work with her, I gain her hide's protection from heat and fire.'

'Excellent. Thank you for explaining it to us.' Dr Brock's tone may have been light but his brow was creased as if he sensed something was amiss. The universal resumed her seat.

'Now to less happy matters,' announced Dr Brock, turning his attention reluctantly away from Connie. 'I must update you on the latest intelligence regarding Kullervo.'

Silence met this announcement. Many looked at the universal to see how she would react to the name of the creature who hunted her, but not Col. He closed his eyes.

Skylark breathed softly in his ear.

'I'm all right,' Col gasped, leaning his forehead against Skylark's white cheek.

Rat nudged him. 'Who's Kullervo?'

'A shape-shifter—our enemy. I'll tell you later.' Col didn't feel like talking about Kullervo just now. He had been the shape-shifter's slave last year—the wounds were still raw.

Alone by the door, Connie gripped her hands together to stop them trembling. She didn't want to hear what Kullervo was doing either and yet it was the only piece of information that really mattered that evening—the real reason why she was here. If he were nearby, if the shape-shifter had slipped back into England, it might explain, might excuse her behaviour.

Dr Brock cleared his throat.

'Kullervo's weather giants have attacked Japan, Malaysia, and Vietnam in recent months. Some five thousand human lives have been lost and up to a hundred thousand people displaced by flooding. Tolls have also been heavy amongst other creatures. One of the last habitats of the three-clawed dragon has been destroyed, as well as the mountain homeland of the moyang melur, a half-human, half-tiger creature.'

An angry buzz ran round the room. Dr Brock held up his hand. 'Our Trustees, with the exception of the representatives of the Elementals, have, of course, gone to the region to lead the counter-attack. I'll keep you all posted on any developments.'

A hand rose from amongst the ranks of the Sea-Snakes, otherwise known as the Company of Sea Creatures and Reptiles.

'Who's that?' muttered Rat, his eye caught by a girl with auburn hair and freckles.

'Jessica Moss, a companion to selkies,' replied Col.

'What are—?'

'Changelings—seals in the sea, people on land. Arran—her companion—is that guy next to her.'

'Yes, Jessica?' Dr Brock said, looking at her over the rim of his glasses.

'Why haven't the Elementals gone?' asked Jessica. 'I would've thought they are needed to help control the weather giants.'

Dr Brock nodded. 'You're right, but unfortunately one of the Trustees, Frederick Cony, was admitted to hospital last week and is unfit to travel. His companion, Gard, the rock dwarf, remains with him at this critical time. Any more questions?'

The room was silent.

'Right,' said Dr Brock with an effort. 'Let's move on to the final item on the agenda. I'll ask Evelyn to update us on matters closer to home.'

Connie's aunt stepped forward. Since she started going out with Mack, she had taken to wearing black biker's gear and tonight had her dark hair tied up in a silver band. Her voice was deep and firm as she commanded the room's attention.

'It won't have escaped your notice that it's crunch time for the environment—we've got to change our ways or global warming will spin out of control. I'm sure you'll agree that we can't sit back waiting for others to provide solutions. Each one of us has to take action.' Col nodded his agreement; he guessed that Evelyn too felt frustrated by the apathy in the Society. 'We on the committee of the Chartmouth

Chapter of the Society want to propose to you that we build the first wind farm in the region, here on Masterson land.'

A murmur of interest rippled round the room as Evelyn beckoned Mr Masterson forward. The farmer patted his companion, a great boar, and then struggled into the centre carrying a model of what looked like a big three-bladed fan.

'Here you are,' he said, 'we're thinking of eight of these on the crest of the hill by the pine plantation.'

'That's right outside my house!' murmured Rat.

'I've already put in for planning permission,' continued the farmer, 'but I'd like to know what you all think before we commit ourselves to the scheme.'

There was a flash of gold and the dragonet Argand flitted out from the ranks of the Sea-Snakes. Connie's special companion creature, the golden dragon had grown over the year to the size of a Labrador with the wingspan of a hang-glider. Rat gasped with admiration as she zoomed around the model, making its blades revolve slowly in the downdraught from her wings.

'You don't mean these exactly, do you, Clive?' prompted Dr Brock.

'No, no,' the farmer laughed, 'I mean eight of these, fifty metres tall.'

Now that was a different matter altogether. Argand veered off into the rafters in alarm. Col felt Skylark shudder. He raised his hand on his mount's behalf.

'But won't they ruin the farm—mess up the sky for winged creatures?' he asked. Other members muttered their agreement, particularly from the eastern side of the room.

'That's why I wanted you all to see it,' Mr Masterson said. 'It won't be an easy decision but that hill's ideal for a wind farm as even on the stillest days it catches the sea breeze—I'm keen to see it go ahead.'

Evelyn noted the concerned faces of the members. 'You need time to think about it, I know,' she said. 'Many of you are upset at the idea of change—only last night my banshees were screaming at me to stop it. But we do need renewable, non-polluting ways of making electricity. We can't ignore reports of how the small degree of warming we've experienced in the last decade has taken its toll. Our creatures are suffering. The frost wolf is already in a steep decline . . .'

Rat gripped Col's arm. 'That's my creature she's talking about, isn't it?'

Col nodded.

'In decline—what does that mean?'

'I think she means that numbers are falling—it might be near extinction.'

'No!' growled Rat. 'We can't let that happen—*I* can't let that happen.' He sat forward, now hanging on every word of the debate.

Down on the floor, Evelyn was still talking. 'We can't turn the clock back to a time before human industrialization. And we can't produce energy without some cost to the environment—I think the inconvenience caused by a wind farm is an acceptable price to pay in the long run.'

29

'Yeah,' muttered Rat, fists clenched on his knees.

Skylark shook his mane angrily. Col could sense the pegasus's annoyance that humans were once more encroaching on what territory was left for the mythical creatures.

'I know it's not a perfect solution but you don't have to decide now,' Evelyn continued, 'the planning decision won't be made until December so there's plenty of time to give us your views. Perhaps some of you might even like to get more involved,' she concluded acidly, casting a significant look at the High Flyers and returning to her seat.

Sensing the dissension building in the room, Dr Brock rose to his feet once more to calm everyone down. 'Well, I think that's enough talking. It's time to enjoy ourselves. Refreshments have been laid on in the lambing shed next door for herbivores. Everyone else is invited to the bonfire in the paddock.'

The crowd began to thin as members drifted away to the feast, arguing furiously the merits of the new idea. Skylark trotted off to the lambing shed to chew the matter over with the other pegasi.

'Come on, let's get Connie,' said Col, pulling Rat to his feet.

They clambered over the bales to where Connie was sitting with her arm around the golden dragon.

'That's an amazing beast you've got there,' said Rat, looking enviously at the dragonet.

'Yes, she is,' Connie replied, her hand rhythmically caressing Argand's golden scales. The dragonet was purring, wisps of smoke curling from her snout. Rat stretched a hand out cautiously and tickled

Argand under the chin; he was rewarded by a purr of pleasure.

'Coming for something to eat?' asked Col.

'No. I'm not hungry,' Connie replied.

Col hunkered down beside her. 'Can we talk?'

Connie glanced up at Rat. 'Not now.'

'So when?' Col pressed.

'I dunno. Soon.'

'You've got to get help.'

Rat's ears pricked up. 'Help with what?'

'It's nothing,' Connie said swiftly, giving Col a warning look.

'Do you know where your aunt's got to?' asked Rat, his eyes searching the crowd of creatures around the bonfire just outside. 'I want to talk to her about the wind farm.'

Connie was glad he had changed the subject. 'I dunno. Look for Mack and you'll find her.'

'Will do.' Rat turned to leave, dragging Col after him. 'Coming, Connie?'

'Later maybe,' she said.

Connie watched them disappear into the crowd. As soon as the two boys were out of sight, Connie slipped out the other way and cycled home alone.

3

Frost Wolf

On the day after the meeting, Connie was sitting on a bench in the school playground, waiting for her friends, Jane and Anneena, to come out of their class. She was trying to concentrate on the ordinary things around her, rather than fret about the night of the storm, but found it impossible to do so. She felt isolated from everyone. Normal life seemed less real than her memories of the beach. Col and Rat were not far away, standing by the school gates in the middle of a gang of boys. Shouts of laughter rose from the group but Connie had no desire to find out what they were up to—she didn't dare go near Col in case he tried to get her to talk again.

'Hey, there you are!'

Connie turned and spotted Jane waving as she and Anneena made a beeline for her. Jane, her blonde hair scraped back in a ponytail, was carrying a pile of serious-looking books. As they got nearer, Connie noticed that Anneena had a thread of gold running through her two long black plaits; not quite in breach of school uniform rules—but nearly.

That was Anneena all over, thought Connie. Pushing the boundaries, taking matters into her own hands.

'Hi there.' Anneena slid onto the bench next to Connie. 'How was biology?'

'Good. It's definitely my best subject.' Connie offered her friends a mint from a tube she took from her pocket. 'Like the hair. What did Mrs Stephens make of it?'

Anneena laughed. 'Oh, you know. She made a bit of a fuss at registration but when I pointed out it wasn't banned in the uniform code, she backed down.' She looked over to Rat who was now climbing on to the narrow top bar of the gate. He balanced there, then threw back his head and howled like a wolf. 'What's he up to?'

'Something he shouldn't,' said Jane matter-of-factly, flicking through her books.

'I've no idea.' Connie frowned, catching Col's eye as he glanced over. He shrugged helplessly: Rat had always been a bit out of control—Col was powerless to stop him celebrating his assessment in his own way.

'Are you OK?' Jane asked, looking up.

'Hmm?'

'Is something wrong?'

Connie shook her head. 'No, I'm fine.'

Anneena now joined in. 'You look tired. Not worrying about your aunt and Mack, are you?'

'No, it's nothing to do with them.'

Anneena pounced on this unspoken confession. 'So there is something!' She paused, as if expecting Connie to blurt out her secrets immediately and seemed rather offended when Connie remained silent. 'You can trust us, you know.'

'I know I can. But really, it's nothing.' Except the fact that she'd raised a storm at the weekend and still did not know how she'd done it.

'Connie,' Jane said gently, laying a hand on her wrist, 'Annie and I did wonder if—now don't fly off the handle when I say this—if all those society meetings might not be doing you any good.'

Connie felt a flutter in her stomach. 'What do you mean?'

Anneena took over again. 'Well, we've been thinking about it for some time now—since your Aunt Godiva suddenly changed personality and dashed off to save the Brazilian rainforest—and we've been wondering what the society really gets up to. You're so secretive about what you do—Col's the same—and now Rat's gone and joined.' Rather unhelpfully, Rat decided at this exact moment to repeat his werewolf impression. Anneena smiled. 'Point made, I think. You can't blame us for wondering.'

Connie groaned inwardly. She hated deflecting questions about the Society; Col was much better at this kind of conversation.

'So tell us. Is the society . . . well, is it safe?'

Connie gave a strangled laugh.

Anneena frowned. 'Look, you've got to admit that the people you mix with are a bit freaky—apart from Col, of course.' They all looked across at Col, the most popular person in their year, who was shaking his head in despair as Rat loped along the wall.

'They're not so strange once you get to understand them,' said Connie quietly.

Connie was saved from further questions by the intervention of the headteacher. Mr Conrad burst from the school and rushed down the drive, his black jacket flapping behind him.

'Uh oh,' said Anneena.

The boys scattered like crows, leaving Rat perched on the top of the gate with Col trying to help him down.

'Sean Ratcliff, what do you think you are doing?' bellowed Mr Conrad. 'Climbing on school buildings is strictly forbidden!'

Connie could see Col tugging surreptitiously at Rat's foot in an attempt to get him down. He managed to topple Rat so that he half-fell, half-slithered to the ground—on top of the teacher.

'Sorry!' muttered Col as he offered Mr Conrad a hand to get up.

'And what was your part in this, Col Clamworthy?' The headmaster rounded on Col as he brushed himself down. 'Why was Sean howling like that? Did you put him up to it?'

Col said nothing, but looked down and scuffed his feet in the dirt.

'Come with me to my office, the pair of you.' Mr Conrad turned on his heel and swept back indoors, Col trailing despondently behind him, but Rat sauntering along as if there was nothing he liked better than being told off by the headmaster.

Mind you, with a tiger of a mother like his, Connie thought, the headmaster must seem a real pussycat.

'Have you ever met anyone like Rat?' Anneena exclaimed, her voice tinged with admiration at his disregard for authority.

'Nope,' Connie admitted.

'Just as well. I don't think Chartmouth could cope with two of them,' said Jane.

Next lesson, Col and Rat arrived late. Rat took the seat next to Connie, dislodging her maths book onto the floor as he spread out his stuff. He scooped her book up with a grin.

'What happened?' Connie whispered.

'Oh, nothing much,' Rat said airily.

'Detention!' growled Col from the other side. 'And I'll miss football practice.'

'Forget it,' Rat continued cheerfully. 'There's more important things to think about than that. Here, Connie, read this!' He pushed a letter from the Society in front of her.

'What!' exclaimed Connie, quickly hiding it on her lap before Mrs Stephens noticed. 'You can't bring this kind of thing into school! What if someone finds it?'

Rat shrugged. 'They won't. No one's interested in what I get up to.'

'I wouldn't be so sure,' muttered Connie, remembering Anneena's and Jane's questions. All the same, she couldn't resist sneaking a look at the letter when Mrs Stephens had her back turned.

'See—my mental's coming this weekend,' said Rat, pointing to the last paragraph.

'Mentor,' Col corrected in an undertone.

'Yeah—Erik Ulvsen—from Norway.' Rat still wasn't bothering to lower his voice. 'And he's bringing a frost wolf with him.'

'Shh!' hissed Connie, shoving the letter under the desk.

'Are you three intending to do any work today?' Mrs Stephens was standing at Rat's shoulder. 'Or are you going to carry on discussing your weekend plans about—what was it?—a *frost wolf*? I assume that isn't a mathematical term?'

Some girls in the front row sniggered at the teacher's sarcasm.

'No—it's just a brand of snowboard,' Col invented quickly.

'Well, Col, if it hasn't escaped your notice, we're in a maths lesson, not on the ski slopes. Page forty-four—and work silently.'

Mrs Stephens turned away.

'See, I told you,' said Rat, doodling a wolf in the margin of his textbook. 'She wasn't interested.'

The following Saturday, Shaker Row was humming with activity as the wedding preparations entered their final week. Connie felt surplus to requirements so decided to take refuge outside. Leaving Evelyn and Mack arguing over the guest list for the reception, she followed the track from the beach up onto the cliffs. A fresh breeze stirred her hair; the sea was broken into white wave crests, sunlight sparkling off its ever-moving surface; the grass rippled at her feet. Connie felt her spirits lift: it was impossible to be gloomy on such a sunny day as this, an unexpected bonus before winter took hold. The air smelt new-washed, sharp with salt and seaweed.

Striding up onto the headland, she stood looking out across the ocean. On the horizon, a tanker churned its way to the oil refinery at Chartmouth. To her left, she could make out the harbour and roofs of Hescombe; to her right, the moors began. A line of dark trees marked the margin of the plantation. She had a good view of the field in front: that was where the wind farm would be, if Mr Masterson got his way. She would see it twirling restlessly on the horizon every time she walked in this direction—man's technology planted in a place that until now had felt peaceful and untamed. Was it right to impose this on the countryside to satisfy human appetite for energy? She remembered Evelyn's words about everything coming at a price. There seemed no easy answer. As if to remind her of their rival claim to the air, seabirds called overhead, displaying their flying skills to the universal as they swept in and out of each other's path in interlocking figures of eight.

Connie sat down in the shelter of a thick mat of brambles that spilled over a bank. Dried blackberries still clung to some of the tendrils. Mottled, blackened leaves rattled in the breeze. The year was getting old, ready to settle down into its winter sleep.

'Universal, he is dead.'

Jolted from her thoughts which were flying up among the birds, Connie looked behind her to see who had spoken. She then realized that the voice had been in her head. She knew that voice: Gard, the rock dwarf, could locate her anywhere in the world as long as her feet were in contact with the ground. Burrowing into the earth through their bond, Connie sought him out.

'Who is dead, Gard?' she asked.

'My companion. Frederick died this morning as the sun rose. He went peacefully in his sleep.'

Connie sensed the rock dwarf's deep pain: though he had seen many companions come and go, he never found the parting from them any easier.

'I'm so sorry,' Connie whispered. 'I don't know what to say.'

The earth seemed to sigh and groan under her, oppressed by this new burden of grief.

'All that he was will remain as part of me, a treasured layer of memory, but already there is no trace of his living presence on the earth. The ground misses his footprint.'

Connie found she was crying for Gard. 'Oh, Gard, what can I do for you?'

'Nothing, Universal. It is enough that you are with me.'

They sat together, linked by the earth that sustained them both, though many miles apart. Connie knew that Gard had the strength of the earth to draw on; his sorrow would chisel new depths in his being, like a sculptor revealing the beauty of the hidden shape within the rock. But the painful process had only just begun. For now they both needed the comfort of each other.

'You mortals are strange creatures,' Gard said at length. 'My destiny lies here, but when your body dies, it seems that your spirit goes elsewhere, beyond my knowledge. I can never follow my companions there.'

The thought of that eternal parting was almost too painful for Connie to contemplate—she would hate to be separated from Argand even for a few days. 'And what will you do now your companion is gone?' she asked gently.

'Resign as a Trustee. Wait for the birth of a new companion. Bide my time.'

'Do you have to resign?'

'Of course—a Trustee cannot hold his position without his companion. It has always been so.'

'You'll not disappear completely, will you, Gard?' Connie asked anxiously.

'Of course not. We can keep in touch—by touch.'

Connie laughed sadly. It was a comfort to know that she was never truly separated from her friend. 'I'll hold you to that.'

'Goodbye, Universal.'

'Goodbye for now, Gard.'

Returning from the deep places of the earth to the bright light of its surface, Connie saw that the sparkling day had clouded over and a chill wind was blowing. Shivering, she got to her feet and headed back to Shaker Row.

Up at the Mastersons' farm, Col and Rat were waiting in the yard for Rat's mentor to arrive. Erik Ulvsen

40

was a distant cousin of Mr Masterson, so the farmer had gone to fetch him himself from the airport for what was expected to be a prolonged Christmas visit while Erik trained Rat in the basics of frost wolf companionship.

'What d'you think he's going to be like?' Rat asked, kicking the muddy tyres of a tractor parked by the barn.

'I dunno,' replied Col, wishing he could be more helpful. He remembered only too clearly his own wait for his first encounter. He was hoping that Erik would not be too much like his cousin as Col found Mr Masterson a bit of a bore—or should that be boar? 'Captain Graves, my mentor, seemed a bit strange to begin with—but he knows his stuff and we get on OK. To be honest, I was more worried that Skylark would reject me. Aren't you a bit anxious about your wolf?'

Rat shook his head. 'No—I get on fine with animals: it's people that I find a problem.'

Mr Masterson's Land Rover bumped into the yard, two men in the front. Col glanced over at Rat: he had gone still, like an animal at bay. The passenger door opened and Erik Ulvsen got out. Col's first impression was that the mentor was very tall—his height accentuated by a long grey coat that skimmed his heels. He had a short crop of spiky blond hair and a silver earring in one ear. Col guessed that he was no older than thirty but it was hard to tell—the mentor's face was weathered into fine lines around the eyes and mouth, the likely result of spending so much time outside in the snow in the sun's glare. When Erik Ulvsen turned to the boys, Col caught a glimpse of keen blue eyes. Erik strode towards them, his coat flapping open, revealing its blood-red lining.

'So which is the boy, then?' With only a hint of a Scandinavian accent, the mentor's voice was surprisingly soft for such a big man. Somehow you felt everything he had to say was of value, making you listen all the harder. He looked expectantly between Col and Rat. 'Let me guess: it is you—am I right?' He pointed at Rat, who nodded as if mesmerized.

Col nudged Rat forward. He had warned him to expect a pep talk from his mentor as Captain Graves had given him the first time—some sober words about the importance of his new responsibilities.

'Hello, I am Erik. What's your name?' The Norwegian held out his hand.

'Sean Ratcliff.' Rat shook hands.

Erik held the grip for a moment longer. 'Really— is that what you like to be called?'

'No, I'm Rat.'

'So, are you ready, Rat?'

Rat nodded cautiously.

Erik smiled, his eyes wrinkling at the corner into deep lines. 'I am about to introduce you to the most amazing creature you will ever meet—no one can be ready for that.'

Mr Masterson arrived at his cousin's elbow. 'Don't you want to put your feet up after your journey, Erik?' he asked. 'I'm sure Rat wouldn't mind waiting till tomorrow.'

Erik had not broken eye contact with Rat; it was

as if they were communicating on a level other than words. 'No, Clive, I think that Rat should not wait a moment longer. We may not have much time left with the frost wolves.'

'But you're not . . . not in the farmyard, surely?' blustered Mr Masterson. 'I've got ewes in the back field, for heaven's sake!'

'They will not disturb us.'

'That's not what I meant!'

Erik seemed not to be listening. He turned away from them all and looked round the yard. 'Follow me,' he told Rat, leading the way to the north side of the barn. 'The frost lingers longest in the shade— that is what he likes best.' He knelt and touched an icy patch of earth. 'This will do. Now watch.'

'You've got a frost wolf with you?' asked Rat in awe.

'Certainly. One of the younger wolves from our pack volunteered for the adventure. He should have reached here by now.'

'How did he travel?' asked Col.

'By air, like me.' Erik gave an almost wolfish grin, teeth showing. 'Well, perhaps not exactly like me. Watch now.'

He bent over the patch of frost and touched it with a finger. Next he scraped a little onto his skin, lifted it to his lips and licked. With the ice still melting on his tongue, he bent his head back and let out a howl. The call echoed from the surrounding hillsides until it sounded as if there were wolves all around them. He stopped—but the howling continued. A chill wind picked up, spinning wisps of straw across the ground.

Mr Masterson was shaking his head in despair as the sheep in the nearest fold scattered; but Rat was alert, his eyes fixed on something that Col could not yet see. He was gazing at a spot right in the centre of the yard. A patch of swirling snow had appeared from nowhere, twisting like a mini tornado. Col and Rat watched in amazement as a shape formed: first paws, then snout, shaking itself free of the wind. Finally, the creature bounded forward, sweeping the remaining snow up into a long feathery tail. A huge frost wolf, Skylark's equal in size, now stood in the centre of the farmyard—white coat glinting like the dazzle of sun on snow, jaws open in a pant, black-rimmed gums and pink tongue showing. Each step the beast took made the ground crackle as he left a trail of frost footmarks. Every breath produced a plume of freezing white vapour that coated all it touched with a dusting of rime. A pair of ice-blue eyes sparkled dangerously as they surveyed the fleeing sheep before turning to the boys.

Col took a step back, knowing better than to get in the way of a creature and its companion. Rat moved slowly forward, hand outstretched. He was making low growling sounds in his throat, following his instinct.

Erik nodded. 'That's right, Rat. Let him smell you. If he likes your scent then you will be accepted.'

'And if he doesn't?' muttered Mr Masterson anxiously.

Rat paused as the wolf loped forward. His hand looked no more than a tiny nip for those massive jaws. The wolf lowered his snout, sniffed—then bounded forward, knocking Rat to the ground.

'No!' shouted Col. It must have gone wrong—the beast was attacking his friend!

He felt a hand grip the back of his jacket. 'Wait!' said Erik, though he too seemed tense.

The frost wolf had one paw on Rat's chest and was staring into his face; Rat looked scared but he met the gaze unflinchingly. There was a pause and then the wolf decided the boy passed inspection: he began licking Rat's face lavishly. He went down on his belly so that boy and wolf could roll over in a play fight. Col had to stop himself intervening—Rat seemed so small between the giant creature's paws and some of the nips looked painful.

'Forgive Icefen—he is really still only a cub,' Erik said as he watched the two scuffle.

'I've never seen a frost wolf before—he's quite something,' Col murmured.

'Yes, he is. Though Icefen is small for his age, of course. You should see the whole pack when it is gathered.'

'And what are his powers—I mean, what can he do?'

Erik pointed. 'You see the frost breath?'

Col nodded: the old tractor parked at the north end of the yard was white with it.

'If a frost wolf breathes on you, you go cold. Two breaths and you will fall asleep—a sensation like what happens to humans caught in the snow. The forgetfulness of exposure, dangerous but effective for getting out of trouble.'

'And a third breath?'

'Frostbite sets in.'

Col gulped, seeing his friend tumbling on the ground with the creature. 'But Rat'll be OK, won't he?'

'Yes, he has the companion's immunity when he is bonded with Icefen. He has nothing to fear—in fact, I suspect he is having the time of his life. I sense already that he is an exceptionally strong companion.'

'Yeah, Connie's always said so.'

'The universal? Now, there is someone I would like to meet. Icefen too.'

'I'm sure you will. She's about the place somewhere. But she keeps away from first encounters in case she messes it up for the new members,' Col explained.

'In that case, we look forward to seeing her later.' Erik gave a piercing whistle and Icefen leapt away from Rat. 'Time for your ride, Rat. Climb on.'

Needing no more encouragement, Rat scrambled onto Icefen, fists gripping the thick fur at the back of the wolf's neck. Icefen gave an excited yip.

'Off you go,' said Erik.

With a whoop and a bark, Rat and Icefen bounded away up the hillside, sheep scattering before them like skittles in a bowling alley.

Mr Masterson turned on his cousin. 'Stop them! That creature will kill my sheep!'

'Calm down, Clive!' Erik said, shading his eyes to follow his pupil's progress. 'Icefen ate two goats this morning before we left home. He won't be hungry again today.'

4
Wedding

A few days later, Col was sluggishly eating his breakfast, reluctant to face another day at school. The night before, Evelyn had brought round the model of the wind farm for them to see; it sat on the table in front of him, looking just as bad as he had feared. The pegasi and the High Flyers were going to be horrified when they saw it at the next Society meeting as even on this small scale it was clear that the huge turbines would make that bit of coast a no-fly zone. Rat and Erik Ulvsen were all for it, of course: they acted as if wind power was all that stood between the frost wolves and extinction; Rat had been going on at Col about it for days now—another reason not to want to go to school.

'Strange how you can't get up during the week but have no problems at the weekend when Skylark's waiting for you,' his grandmother observed acerbically as she buttered herself some toast. Col grinned at her.

There was a scuffling at the front door and then a thump as the post fell onto the mat in the hallway.

'Get them for me, will you, dear,' Mrs Clamworthy asked when her grandson showed no signs of moving.

Col took a big mouthful of cereal and crunched it as he went to fetch the letters. Among the usual pile of junk mail lay a thick brown envelope with the initials SPMC stamped across the top.

'There's something for you from the Society,' he said as he dropped the mail onto her lap. Mrs Clamworthy rifled through until she found the brown envelope and slit it open with her knife. Putting her glasses on, she read the contents carefully twice through. Col returned to his breakfast and waited for her to say something.

'So, what's it about then?' he prompted, curious as to why the Society was writing to her and not to him.

'The poor man's not been dead a week and they're already filling his shoes,' she said angrily, handing the letter to her grandson to read for himself.

Col took the papers and looked them over. The first page announced the death of Frederick Cony, Trustee for the Elementals, and the subsequent retirement of his companion, Gard. The letter, which was addressed to the worldwide membership of the Company of Creatures of the Four Elements, went on to announce the holding of elections to fill the vacant positions. A list of candidates followed with a separate sheet for each pair to set out their manifestos.

'I see what you mean,' Col said as he leafed through the candidates' details.

'They say it's because of the Far Eastern crisis,' Mrs Clamworthy said, wrinkling her nose in disdain, 'but I think it's all that Coddrington's doing. He's been itching to stand for election ever since Frederick's health began to fail.'

Col looked back at the list of candidates. After Lee Chan and his companion, Jade, a rock dwarf, were listed Ivor Coddrington and Hoo, the weather giant. He pulled out the pair's manifesto and read it with growing incredulity:

'Ivor Coddrington has been a key member of the British section of the Society for the Protection of Mythical Creatures since 1976. He is one of only five companions to weather giants in the world, making his skills much sought after and particularly crucial at this time when the earth is under attack by some of these creatures. He was also instrumental in the identification of the Society's only universal companion and has remained closely involved with her training. In the last two years he has also played a major role in protecting the universal from attacks by Kullervo.'

'I see he doesn't mention that he turned Connie down, does he?' Col said with a disgusted laugh. '"Closely involved"—well, if that includes spying, I s'pose it's true, though from what I've seen, no one's been helping Connie with her training. And as for his "major role" in saving her, I don't remember seeing him on the cliff edge at Deadman's Cove or up Merlin's Oak.'

49

'I know, dear. He's quite a horrid little man.'

'Your Company would be mad to elect him.'

'Exactly. But most of the people voting don't know him.' She folded the letter up thoughtfully and tucked it inside her knitting bag.

'So when will the result be known?'

'Just before Christmas. We have two weeks to return our voting slips.'

Col pushed his cereal aside. 'Well, reading that has put me off my breakfast. I hope Connie doesn't get to see it. She'll be furious that he even mentioned her. She's depressed enough already as it is.'

'So I've noticed. What do you think's wrong with her?'

'She's . . .' This couldn't go on—Connie really had to tell someone. 'She's worried about something.'

'Did she say what it was?'

Col wanted to tell her but knew it shouldn't be his decision. 'Not sure.'

'I wouldn't be surprised if it wasn't the wedding. I'm a little worried, if the truth be known. My son is a wonderful man but even I recognize he is not the easiest of people to live with.'

Col glanced at the clock and realized he would miss the bus if he didn't hurry.

'Gotta go!' he said, leaping up from the table to pull on his jacket.

'That hair of yours hasn't seen a comb for a week!' his grandmother called after him.

'No point—I'm off flying after school!' He hopped into his trainers on his way out.

'You're just like your father was at your age!' his grandmother said in exasperation.

'I hope not!' Col yelled, waving goodbye as he jogged off down the road.

At lunchtime, Col cornered Connie by the drinks machine. This could not wait any longer.

'Look, Connie, we've got to tell someone.'

She fumbled with her purse, pretending not to hear. 'Have you got ten p?'

He dug in his pocket and handed her a coin. 'You know what I'm talking about.'

A carton of juice clunked into the bottom of the machine. Connie knelt down to retrieve it. 'It was nothing.'

'Don't talk rubbish—we both know something really bad happened that night. You can't act as if it doesn't matter.'

Connie stabbed the straw through the hole at the top of the carton.

'Gran was asking after you—and I'm sure Dr Brock suspects something.' Col was beginning to be annoyed by her lack of response. Didn't she realize how serious this was? She was acting as if she could ignore the problem and it would go away. 'If you don't say something, I'll have to!'

'You wouldn't!' Connie glared at him. How could he even think of doing that to her? Then they'd all know—they'd all hate her!

'Think how I'm feeling—I know you're in trouble, but hiding the truth will only make it worse! If anything happens again, it'd be my fault.'

'But it might not happen again,' she pleaded desperately. Part of her knew he had a point, but she didn't want to listen.

Col shook his head. 'But you don't know that—I can't know that for sure.'

'Please don't say anything.' She seized on the first excuse she could think of. 'It'll spoil the wedding.'

Col ran his hands through his hair in exasperation. 'Isn't this more important? I'm sure Evelyn would think so. Look, as soon as the wedding's over, you must tell someone, OK?'

'Maybe—when I'm ready.' She crumpled up the carton and threw it in the bin. 'Let's find the others.'

Col trailed after her, feeling bad that he had to bully her like this. He understood why she was panicking—he'd probably feel the same in her place—but he was convinced he was right to press her. She'd end up killing someone—perhaps herself—if she dabbled in storm-raising again.

Out in the playground, they found Rat with Anneena and Jane.

'There you are!' exclaimed Anneena. 'We were wondering where you'd got to. Look at this.'

She handed Connie a clipboard: it was a petition in favour of the wind farm.

Rat bounded onto the bench beside Connie. 'Yeah, I wanted to get involved so Evelyn asked me to collect signatures from kids our age.' He leafed through the pages already filled with names.

'It's a good idea,' said Anneena. 'We've got to show the council that we care about stuff like that. They listened over Mallins Wood—maybe they will again.'

Connie tried to act interested but really her mind was still on the argument with Col. 'So, how many people have signed?'

'Nearly everyone I've asked,' said Rat proudly. 'I even got Mr Conrad to sign during detention, didn't I, Col?'

Col nodded. 'Yeah—though it might just've been to get you to shut up.'

Rat grinned. 'Well, it worked—don't diss the strategy. Not that it always works out like that,' he conceded. 'A few people are still against.' He glanced at Col. 'I think someone's organizing a protest locally.'

'Mr Quick,' supplied Jane as she shuffled through some photos she had taken.

'Who's he?' asked Rat.

'Manager of the oil refinery in Chartmouth—we met him a couple of years ago. Sacked my dad.'

'So I take it he's a nice man?' Rat balanced on the back of the seat.

'Not really. But he does live in Carstones, right below the site of the wind farm.' She found the photo she had been looking for of the little fishing village with its picturesque houses clustered around a bay the other side of the headland from Rat's home. 'Can't blame him for not wanting it on his doorstep,' Jane said fairly.

'I s'pose you can't win them all.' Rat tapped the clipboard on Col's head. 'So, mate, are you going to sign now?'

Col shook it off. 'I still haven't made up my mind. Not everyone I know is in favour.'

Connie and Rat understood that he was referring to Skylark's continued opposition to the scheme. Col's loyalties were divided: as a human, he thought wind farms a good idea; as a companion, he wanted to defend Skylark's territory in the air.

'Go on, Col. Think about my friends for once,' Rat urged. 'Some of us can only survive at low temperatures; Erik told me that a degree or two more warming and they would have to go even further north. I mean what's a little inconvenience compared to extinction?'

Col passed the board back. 'I can't. I'm sorry.'

Rat was beginning to get angry with him. 'Look, if it was the other way round, if it was your companion that was suffering, I'd sign. We need more wind farms—we've got to stop global meltdown.'

Col sighed. 'Of course I agree with that—I'd be mad not to.' Rat shoved the clipboard into his chest; Col pushed it away. 'It's just, why here? Why *this* wind farm in *our* airspace?'

'They've got to go somewhere. Why not here? It's on my doorstep—I'll see it and hear it every time I step outside and am I giving everyone grief about that?' Rat turned to the universal. 'What about you, Connie?'

'Yeah, I'll sign.' Connie decided she had wavered long enough: she was ready to put her name to the scheme. 'I think wind farms are something we're all going to have to learn to live with.'

Rat suppressed an urge to howl in triumph—he had the universal's signature! 'Thanks, Connie—that means a lot to me and my frosty friends,' he said, his grin stretching from ear to ear.

Col felt self-conscious being singled out as the only one of them not to put his name to the petition. He got up and stretched, pretending to be cool about it. 'I think I'll go play football. See you later.'

'What did he mean, he's got friends against it?' asked Anneena, her curiosity piqued by a conversation she hadn't quite understood. 'What friends were you both talking about? I thought *we* were your friends?'

'Col—the Man of Mystery.' Rat put on an American TV announcer's voice and began fooling around. '*Hides his secrets in his secret Society. And he would've gotten away with it, if it hadn't been for you meddlin' kids.*' He tweaked Anneena's plaits.

Connie pulled him away before he did any more damage to Anneena—or the Society.

'What?' Rat asked innocently.

Connie rolled her eyes.

'Look, O-Miss-high-and-mighty Universal, sometimes the best way to hide something is to make it obvious. Anneena likes a mystery—if we make fun of it, she'll lose interest.'

Connie stopped in her tracks and looked back. Anneena was laughing with Jane: it seemed as if their conversation had moved on and she'd forgotten about Col. 'You know, Rat, I think you may be right.'

She just wished she could make Col forget about the storm-raising so easily.

Evelyn and Mack's wedding took place in the register office in Chartmouth town hall that Saturday. It was a small affair with only family and close friends invited. Connie was her aunt's bridesmaid. Evelyn stood beside her, wearing a simple white gown that clung to her slender form like a glove. Her long hair rippled down her back, her only ornament a headdress of red berries, her bouquet a bunch of scarlet roses. Connie had never seen her looking so beautiful. As for herself, she was wearing a red silk dress with a posy of white roses and her hair was caught up in a small circlet of red-berried holly. Mack for once had put aside his leathers and donned a black suit with a white collarless shirt. His best man, a rather astounded-looking Col, was dressed to match.

Col had been surprised to be asked by his father to act as his best man, though the offer had been made in a typically off-hand manner that morning.

'Can you look after the rings for me?' Mack had asked him. 'I can't trust Casey or Digger to remember to turn up.'

Col had decided to take it as a compliment that his dad had entrusted him with this task, even though he had come third on the list of possibles. Standing straight-backed in front of the registrar's desk, he cast a sidelong look at Connie, who was swaying slightly on the other side of her aunt. She would have no more excuses now. He was determined that either she or he should talk to Dr Brock today as soon as the ceremony was over.

'You are now husband and wife,' announced the registrar.

Mack bent down and kissed Evelyn. 'You must be mad to marry me,' he told her when they broke apart.

'I know,' she replied with a laugh.

Mr Masterson had offered his barn for the wedding reception so as many creatures as possible from the Society could come. A band of young musicians from the Sea-Snakes had been hired to provide the entertainment and the dancing was already well under way. Connie watched from a hay-bale as her aunt whirled around in Mack's arms like a white spinning top, her head thrown back in a raucous laugh. Connie could not remember seeing her aunt so happy: whatever others might think of the marriage, Evelyn was clearly content with her choice.

Rat and Col clambered over the rows of bales towards her, balancing plates piled high with food.

'It's mighty craic this,' Rat said through a mouthful of baked potato, nodding over at the dancers. Argand was now darting in and out of the people, making a few of them stumble as she tried to catch up with the end of one line. Skylark lingered longingly at the edge of the dance floor, twitching his ears in time with the music.

Col nudged Connie and nodded towards Dr Brock, who was sitting near the band. 'So, Connie, shall we tell him now?'

Connie opened her mouth to reply but, at that moment, the double doors to the barn burst open, letting in a blast of cold air. Above the music a shrill keening noise could be heard, clashing with the tune, growing louder and louder. Col's jaw dropped as a stream of dark figures poured into the room, their long shaggy hair flying behind them, their ragged, rotting clothes trailing on the ground. Col and Rat stuffed their fingers in their ears; Connie sat rigid, her hands clenched at her sides. The creatures had pale, gaunt faces, grey like mist, and their skin shone with a clammy, cold lustre. Their mouths were open in a constant wail; dark circles of grief. The banshees converged on the centre of the barn, scattering the other dancers, until they had surrounded Mack and Evelyn. The band flagged, the music died away, drowned out by the rise and fall of the banshees' cry. Then, responding to a secret signal, the banshees began to sway from side to side, rolling their heads on their scrawny necks, tossing their hair to and fro in a strange jerking dance. Their wail echoed through the barn like the wind that frets in the chimneys of Dartmoor's isolated houses. Answering their call, Evelyn dropped her hands from Mack's shoulders and began to sway in time with the banshees, flinging her hair from side to side, the berry wreath skittering to the floor to be kicked into the dust by the horny-soled feet of her companions. Mack looked lost.

'Hey, this is wild!' Rat exclaimed. He threw his plate aside and leapt down the terrace of hay-bales onto the floor, mingling with the writhing banshees. Picking up the rhythm, he too began to sway in time with the keening. His move broke the spell that they had all been under. Getting the idea, Mack shrugged and began to copy his wife, at first self-consciously and then letting himself go. Others began to follow suit, stepping nervously back on the floor before allowing the dance to sweep them away. The floor now resembled a forest of trees swaying under a buffeting gale.

Now everyone was distracted, Col decided it was the perfect moment to get Dr Brock on his own. 'Are you coming with me to tell him, Connie?' He stood up.

Connie did not answer. Her face was pale, her eyes closed and her breathing laboured. The wail of the banshees had penetrated her deeply, blowing her off to the lonely places on the moor where they lived, winding her into the sad secrets of blemished lives and sudden deaths that was the lot of many creatures. Their wailing filled her with a hopelessness that was too painful to bear. Grappling for her shield, she raised the protection of the universal over her head and shut out the anguish, fencing herself off from them.

'Connie?'

'No,' she said bitterly, full of self-loathing. 'I don't want anyone to know that I'm . . . I'm like that.'

Col gritted his teeth, hating himself for what he was about to do. 'Well, if you won't, I will.'

He jumped down the bales before she could stop him. Connie watched horror-struck as he approached Dr Brock. She saw them put their heads together, saw Dr Brock turn to look up at her wide-eyed—that was enough.

Getting quickly to her feet, she left the swaying mob of wedding guests and ran outside.

Anger swelled inside Connie as she fled back to her great-uncle's cottage. Too full of feelings to sleep, she climbed to the summit of the hill and took a diversion from the path, recklessly stepping onto the rough grass that led to the very edge of the cliff. Just then she hated Col—but most of all she hated herself. A storm of fear pounded inside her as she recalled Dr Brock's expression.

It was too, too horrible—she had been exposed as a monster, a liar.

She didn't know what to do with herself. If only she could find release for her overcharged emotions! Her skin crackled with power: the feelings seemed to be fizzing out of her—out of her control. Thunder rumbled in the distance; lightning flickered on the horizon. Connie raised her arms above her head and let go, shouting her anger to the storm. A breeze picked up, soon growing into a gale. It whipped up the waves to rise against the base of the cliff, clawing their way towards the universal. Connie stood firm as the wind buffeted her, hair flying like a flag behind her. Clenching her fists at the sky, she pummelled the clouds to drop their load. They obeyed and rain began to lash down, soaking the grass at her feet, icy droplets stinging her cheeks with their kiss. Next, she stabbed her outstretched fingers at the sky and forks of lightning hissed down to their tips, glancing off to the earth so that she became surrounded by a glittering web of light. Darkness welled up inside her and swept her away, plunging her into the storm so that she became one with it.

Down by the cottages a motorbike drove into view.

'Dirty weather brewing,' Dr Brock shouted over his shoulder to Col who was riding pillion. Col did not answer: he was staring at the little figure on the headland illuminated in intense shafts of light. Dr Brock screeched to a halt. 'Holy Moses!' he breathed, spotting what Col had seen.

'What's she doing?' Rat asked, his enthusiastic face peering out of the sidecar. 'What creature's she encountering?'

'Good question,' said Dr Brock, taking off his helmet. 'Is this what you meant, Col, when you told me about that night on the beach?'

'No, not like this—she was asleep when I found her.' Col couldn't believe what he was seeing— Connie creating a thunderstorm. She would get herself killed if she carried on like this! 'We've got to stop her.' Without waiting for the others, he jumped off the bike and began to run at full speed up to the headland. The wind battered him back, trying to prevent him reaching her; hail pinged off his face like shotgun pellets. 'Connie!' he yelled as he climbed up onto the hilltop. 'Connie! Stop it!'

She did not turn. It was doubtful if she could hear him with the noise of the storm howling in her ears.

She was standing on the very edge of the cliff. Col started forward to reach her until he was abruptly pulled back by Dr Brock.

'You can't touch her: you'll be killed!' he shouted in Col's ear.

Col could see now that he was right: Connie was conducting the lightning to glide over the grass, picking off targets to reduce to cinders. A field away a sheepfold exploded apart, a stack of hay-bales scorched and withered.

He yelled again: 'Connie!'

An echo of his cry penetrated her mind. Wrapped in her glittering web, she turned to them, her eyes cold. There he was: the boy who had betrayed her.

Suddenly Col was afraid—that wasn't his friend looking at him.

'Dive!' shouted Dr Brock, pulling Col and Rat to the ground beside him as overhead a lightning bolt whistled past.

'What's she playing at?' Rat protested indignantly.

'She's not playing,' Dr Brock hissed. 'If we stay here, we'll be fried.' He shuffled back on his stomach, beckoning Col and Rat to follow him. But as they beat a hasty retreat, a streak of gold zoomed over, heading straight for Connie. Argand plunged through the mesh of lightning, unharmed by its burning touch, and landed at Connie's feet. Her tongue flickered across Connie's toes. With the suddenness of a switch being flicked, the lightning disappeared and Connie crumpled to the ground, her arms around Argand's neck.

Hesitantly, Col raised his head to check that all was clear and then dashed over to Connie to pull her away from the cliff edge, Dr Brock and Rat in close pursuit.

'What were you doing!' he yelled at her, angry beyond words at the fright she had given them all.

Connie was sobbing, horrified by what she had done. She glanced to her right and found the edge of the cliff only a metre away. With a muffled scream, she scrambled on her hands and knees away from the drop.

'I can't believe it!' Col shouted at her. 'You nearly killed us!'

'Hush!' said Dr Brock, coming to kneel beside Connie. 'Connie, what happened?'

Connie looked from him, to Argand, to the sea now subsiding from its earlier fury, and her sobbing intensified. It was worse than before—far worse—because this time it had been she who had surrendered to the darkness inside her—to the hatred and the anger.

'I'm sorry, so sorry!' she wailed, burying her head in her hands.

Dr Brock gingerly put his arm around her shoulder as if he half expected her to give him an electric shock. 'It's not the first time, is it? Col told me,' he said gently but Connie was now sobbing and shivering so much that she was beyond answering. 'Let's get her inside.' Picking her up in his arms, he carried her back down the path, Argand flying in circles over him. The two boys tagged along, not knowing what to think.

'Come into our kitchen,' Rat said when they arrived back at the cottages. 'My parents will be asleep by now.' He opened the back door for Dr Brock and then ran upstairs to fetch a blanket for Connie. Col switched the kettle on, avoiding looking at her as she lay curled up, shaking, in a corner of the sofa. Wolf padded out of his basket and laid his head in her lap. Her hand fell to rest on his fur and she seemed to calm down a little. Argand placed a possessive paw on her arm, eyeing the dog jealously. Dr Brock stood behind her seat, removed his glasses to rub his eyes as he tried to make sense of the night's events.

'You must tell me, Connie: what happened just then?' he asked softly but with a firmness that showed he was determined to get an answer.

Connie gulped, her face a mass of straggling hair, streaming eyes, and blotched cheeks. 'I was angry. I . . . I saw Col talking to you. I ran away but then the anger just seemed to take over—I couldn't stop myself once I started. I summoned the storm.'

'And did you see us?' he asked, coming to sit in a chair opposite her and taking her hand in his.

'Yes, but once the storm gripped me, it felt as if you didn't really matter—as if you were nothing more than those sheepfolds I destroyed. I'm so, so sorry!'

'I know you are—but we've got a problem, haven't we?'

She nodded miserably. 'I've been so scared! The first time it happened I was asleep—now I'm doing it when I'm awake! I don't know what's happening to me. I can't sleep—I can't be trusted.' Her shoulders began to heave as she was racked by new sobs.

'There, there,' he said gently, patting her hand, but his face was drawn with anxiety. 'Something's clearly gone seriously wrong with Connie's gift,' he said at length when no one else spoke. 'I think we'd better inform the Trustees and ask them to help us. I don't know what else to suggest. But you'll have to sleep, Connie. I think we should risk having Argand staying at Hugh's with you tonight under the covers: she'll make sure you don't go wandering again.' He gave Connie's hand a final squeeze before releasing it. 'There's nothing more we can do now. I think it's time we all went to bed.'

Having seen Connie back to her house, Col and Dr Brock remounted the motorbike. From the grim silence Dr Brock maintained on the way back to Hescombe, Col doubted that either of them would sleep much tonight when they did reach their beds.

5
New Trustee

'I don't believe it!' Mrs Clamworthy exclaimed as she ripped open the envelope containing the latest missive from the Society. 'They didn't!'

'Didn't what?' Col asked distractedly. He was looking at the Wednesday edition of the local newspaper, wondering what they had made of Saturday night's sudden squall. The reporter had collated local reactions to the 'funny weather' Hescombe had been experiencing of late, looking for explanations for the microclimatic phenomenon. Col did not find the weather very 'funny' himself; he was still shaken by what had happened on the headland. He did not know how to talk to Connie when he saw her at school—after all, she had tried to kill him.

'They've only gone and elected Ivor Coddrington and Hoo, the weather giant, to be Trustees! It was a landslide victory—the right man for the moment and all that rubbish.'

'No! That's bad.' The news jolted Col away from his thoughts. His gran looked really upset. 'I s'pose there's a bright side,' he said, trying to cheer her. 'They're bound to send him off to the Far East to chase weather giants. We might be better off not having him on our backs the whole time.'

'Humph!' Mrs Clamworthy said, not being so optimistic. 'I'm ashamed to be an Elemental this morning.'

'Oh, don't say that, Gran,' said Col, putting the paper down. 'Look, why don't you go and see the water sprites today? That always makes you feel better.'

'Perhaps I will.' She glanced up at the clock. 'Shouldn't you get a move on? You'll miss the bus and your father's not around to give you a lift, remember!'

As the bus pulled up at the school gates, Col saw Hugh Lionheart driving off having just dropped Connie and Rat. Connie walked in on her own, but Rat lingered, on the lookout for Col.

'Hi!' Rat shouted as his friend jumped off the bus.

'Hey, Rat, not talking to Connie?' asked Col.

'Nah,' said Rat as he watched Connie disappear into the school. 'Are you?'

Col grimaced.

'I told her on Monday,' Rat continued, 'that she should just admit that she'd been showing off with that lightning bolt. I mean I'd've done the same if I could do all that stuff—amazing. But she's still in a mood about it.'

'Perhaps she really couldn't help it,' suggested Col cautiously, already knowing his friend's thoughts on this subject. 'Perhaps she's telling the truth when she said something kind of took over.'

'Oh yeah? "I blast you to bits but I don't know I'm doing it,"' replied Rat, giving a cruelly accurate impression of Connie's high voice. 'Pull the other one, it's got bells on. She had her eyes open the whole time. She knew what she was doing.'

'Look, Rat, Connie doesn't tell lies—it's not like her.'

'Yeah, well, perhaps we're just beginning to learn what she's really like. I mean, did you know she could do that? It's nothing to be ashamed of having awesome powers—I'm dead jealous—but why doesn't she just admit it to us, her friends?'

'But that's not how she thinks.'

A bell rang inside.

'Come on,' said Rat who was rarely so eager to get to class. 'Last day of term—they won't expect us to do any work surely?'

Connie sat on her own for the carol service in the school hall two rows away from Rat and Col. She could not bear to look at them as she felt so ashamed of what she had done. It was torture sharing the car with Rat on the way to school; every moment spent in the same class agonizing: she didn't know if she could bear it any longer. She would have to keep away from them.

Jane and Anneena came in to the hall with their class and took seats next to her. Jane gave her a hesitant smile.

'Are you all right?' she asked. 'You look upset.'

'I'm fine,' lied Connie.

The choir shuffled into place and the soloist stepped forward to sing the first verse of the opening carol. Watching him command the attention of the whole school prompted Connie to ask herself if she did not secretly enjoy creating the storms? She could certainly remember in snatches the exhilaration of directing the lightning, standing at the epicentre of the elements, bending them to her will. It was all a mystery to her, not least because she could not say which mythical creature's powers she had been channelling to summon the storm. If she knew that, then at least she might be better prepared to resist it.

Whatever was going on, her training had released something dangerous in her that she could not fully control. This had culminated in her almost killing Col, Rat, and Dr Brock: she could not afford to let it happen again. Her hopes now rested on the Trustees; she was convinced that they were bound to come up with a rescue plan.

'What're you doing for the holidays?' Anneena whispered during a pause in the singing.

'Not much. Staying with Uncle Hugh,' Connie replied. 'You?'

'My sister and her husband are over. We're having a party tonight, but I don't s'pose you can come?'

'Yeah, I'm free.'

'I thought you'd be busy with your society thing?'

'I'm having a break from that at the moment.' Connie's cheeks reddened.

'So you're not going to the meeting with Rat and Col? They said they were tied up tonight.'

Meeting? What meeting? Connie glanced anxiously over at the two boys. Col was looking grimly at the stage but she had the impression that he had just turned his gaze from her.

'No, I've not been invited to that.' But she could guess that her name would be much mentioned in her absence. Her actions had to have consequences— but just what they would be she could not guess. This was only the beginning.

The Chartmouth Chapter met as usual in the Mastersons' barn. Unlike the upbeat mood of the AGM, this emergency meeting began in a sombre atmosphere. Dr Brock took the floor to explain to the members what had happened.

'As many of you will know by now, last Saturday night the universal was responsible for extensive storm damage to the coastline just south of here, near the site of the proposed wind farm. According to her own account, this was the second occasion that she had summoned a storm—though both times, she appears to have not been fully in control of her actions.'

Rat snorted sceptically, provoking Skylark to whinny on the other side of Col. The pegasus was incensed that anyone should doubt Connie. The two were already at odds over the wind farm, so the dispute over Connie was making the rift wider. The majority of Society members had come out in favour of the wind power scheme, much to Skylark's disgust. Col felt torn in two, his loyalty divided between his friends. Just now it felt as if everything was going wrong.

'Now, I have taken it upon myself to write to the Trustees explaining the situation,' continued Dr Brock. 'When I phoned Headquarters yesterday they promised they would be sending someone down here to help us this evening. With any luck, they should be arriving shortly.'

'Who are they sending?' asked Mrs Clamworthy.

'I don't know. In the absence of the Trustees abroad, I suggested a unicorn and companion as they are experienced in sleep problems.'

'Well, that's not going to get to the heart of the matter,' interrupted Captain Graves. 'This isn't about sleep. The girl's a danger to herself and others asleep or awake—we need to know what's going on before someone gets killed.'

'We've always known that Connie's gift is dangerous, Michael,' said Dr Brock. 'I think our job is to help her get her training back on course so that she can direct it safely.'

'Our first priority must be to stop people getting killed!' Captain Graves countered, gesturing at Col and Rat with his cane. 'You can't hide from us that you're all very lucky to be here today. I don't want the Society's best young pegasus rider to be reduced to a pile of ash.'

'No one wants that,' Dr Brock said wearily.

There was a loud cough by the door to the barn.

'May I come in?'

Ivor Coddrington was standing at the entrance waiting for someone to notice his arrival.

'Oh, Ivor,' said Dr Brock, trying to summon some enthusiasm to greet him. 'What brings you here?'

Mr Coddrington gave a modest bow. 'In the absence of my fellow Trustees, I have been appointed to come and sort out your little problem.'

'Not exactly a *little* problem, I'm afraid,' said Mr Masterson, conducting him to a chair at the front of the Elementals. 'We've a rogue universal on the loose.'

'Hardly!' tutted Mrs Clamworthy, bridling at the description.

Mr Coddrington sat down, crossed his long, spindly legs, cracked his knuckles and looked up at the gathering attentively. He seemed to be waiting for something.

'Oh, and . . . er . . . congratulations on your election, Ivor,' Dr Brock said heavily.

'Thank you,' Mr Coddrington replied with evident satisfaction. 'I'll endeavour to serve to my best ability.'

'Considerable ability, you should say,' butted in Mr Masterson, looking proudly at his daughter's mentor, feeling the honour reflected well on his family. The new Trustee smiled slightly, waving the compliment away with a white hand.

'I've been listening to what you've been saying, and I've read your chairman's report,' Mr Coddrington continued, nodding to Dr Brock. 'It seems to me that we need to launch an investigation, interview relevant witnesses, and the accused herself, of course, before taking action.

72

'Accused!' Mrs Clamworthy interrupted. 'Connie is not accused of anything; she needs help.'

'We can help her by judging the case against her impartially. Despite the undoubted uniqueness of her gift, we cannot treat the universal any differently to any other member of the Society caught undertaking such reckless—dare I say, murderous—acts. We have procedures. My first task as a new Trustee will be to see that these procedures are followed. And therefore I have, as I have already said, taken the decision to launch an inquiry. She will have her chance to put forward her defence; just as you will all have your opportunity to give your views. The process will be transparent and fair to all concerned.'

There was a murmur of approval from some of the members but Dr Brock now looked extremely worried.

'But, Ivor, when we asked for help we did not mean that Connie should be put on trial. We wanted to get to the bottom of the problem and help her overcome it.'

'And we will be getting to the bottom of the problem, believe me,' said Mr Coddrington.

'But I'm not sure we will agree to let this happen to one of our members.' Dr Brock looked around the room hoping to find some support from his colleagues. Some of the heads nodded, but around half of those gathered sat with stony faces.

'Well, that's as may be, but I think you'll find that the rules say that, because of their rarity and importance to the Society, matters to do with universals fall into the competence of the chief governing body, in other words, of the Trustees.'

'And I suppose you checked the rules before coming down here?' said Dr Brock tersely.

'Indeed I did.'

Col was seething. They could not surrender Connie up to this man like a prisoner.

'And what are you going to do to her?' he blurted out. Mr Coddrington turned to see the boy's face taut with suppressed anger.

'Colin Clamworthy, isn't it?'

'That's right,' he replied defiantly, his chin up.

'A friend of the universal, if I remember correctly.'

'Yes.'

'A friend she tried to kill last weekend.'

Col lowered his eyes. 'I don't know about that . . .'

'Don't you think that for her sake, as well as yours, we need to stop her?'

Col said nothing. Of course she had to be stopped—but not like this.

'I've always said that the universal gift was a threat to the Society—and now here we have the evidence. Well-intentioned though Miss Lionheart undoubtedly is—or was—she has sown the wind and is reaping the whirlwind—if you forgive my rather apt expression.'

'Hear, hear,' muttered Mr Masterson.

'Unfortunately, my advice that she should only be allowed to practise within safe limits was ignored by my colleagues,' Mr Coddrington continued with a sad shake of his head. 'They unleashed her on the universal's reading room with no idea of what might follow. Who

74

knows what secrets the universals have been hiding away from the rest of us up there? Do any of us hide our professional knowledge from others? No. We all read in the open—train in the open. The universals conceal themselves away from the rest of us. It can't be good for people with such powers to be allowed to exercise them with no controls, no oversight.' Mr Coddrington rose to his feet and punched one fist into his open palm for emphasis. 'Well, what I want to say to you is that it stops here and stops now. I will do my duty by the Society and ensure that this abuse of power is not allowed to continue!'

'But, Ivor,' Dr Brock protested, 'that sounds all very well on the hustings, but we are dealing with a child. This is the first hiccup in her training she's met. We must not throw the baby out with the bathwater and rush to extreme measures.'

'First hiccup?' Mr Coddrington said incredulously. 'So being captured twice by Kullervo, nearly exposing the Society to the world last year, these were nothing, were they?'

'You know full well that these things were not Connie's fault.'

'No, I do not know that. The events of last year showed a dangerous wilfulness on the girl's part. I am yet to be convinced that this same wilfulness is not now causing the storms.'

'But—!'

'No buts, Francis, I am overruling you on this. The inquiry is to start immediately. Tonight, I will interview each of you who were present on the headland and I'll see the universal tomorrow. We cannot hang around wringing our hands on this issue: decisive action is required. So if you will play your part and ensure that she turns up here in the morning, I will then do mine.' He paused for breath. 'As she's not legally of age, she should be accompanied by a responsible adult—her aunt, I suppose.' He looked round the room for Evelyn.

'She's out of contact—on honeymoon,' said Dr Brock quietly.

'Oh yes,' Mr Coddrington said with a knowing smile, 'with the Kraken companion. I remember entering it in my records last week. Well, someone else then.'

'I'll bring her,' said Dr Brock.

'Good. Right, to whom shall I speak first?'

Col waited outside the dining room door in the Mastersons' house, sitting on the bottom step of the stairs. The hall was cold and smelt of the pile of farm wellingtons stacked by the front door. From the murmur of voices inside, he knew that Mr Coddrington was still questioning Rat and taking much longer with him than he had for Col's interview. That did not bode well. Col felt terrible that he had been the one who had started all this by making Connie's problem public.

Dr Brock came in from the kitchen carrying a mug of cocoa.

'Here, drink this,' he said, handing it to Col.

'Thanks,' Col replied, staring miserably down into the swirling contents.

'It's my fault, you know,' Dr Brock said, sitting down beside him, his wrinkled face somehow seeming much older tonight. 'I should have seen this coming a mile off. Ivor's been against Connie from the beginning. Of course the first thing he would do with his power is seek to use it against her and we handed him the opportunity on a plate.'

The door opened and Rat came out looking bemused. It snapped shut again behind him.

'What did you say to him?' Col asked angrily.

'Keep your hair on,' said Rat. 'I told him the truth, of course. I told him what we saw.'

'And did you tell him what you said to Connie on Monday?' Col pressed him. Dr Brock looked up, not having heard about Rat's falling out with Connie.

'Well, he did get it out of me, yeah,' said Rat, wrinkling his nose. 'Creep, isn't he? Are all your Society people like that?'

Col brushed aside the question. 'Well you've gone and done it now!' He jumped up, slopping the cocoa onto the carpet.

'Done what? I just told him the truth, all right?' Rat squared up to Col, fists clenched. 'Anyway, why blame me? You were the one who told on her in the first place, weren't you? She wouldn't't've been so angry that night if you'd kept your mouth shut!'

'Now, boys, boys!' said Dr Brock, barging between them. 'You've been put in an impossible position tonight. You mustn't come to blows over it: we've got enough problems to deal with as it is. Col, Rat's right to tell the truth; Rat, Col is right to want to

77

protect Connie: you don't understand the man we're dealing with as he does.'

The dining room door opened again and Mr Coddrington strode out looking immensely pleased with himself. He stopped short on seeing them huddled outside.

'Oh, didn't I make myself clear?' he said, his manner lordly. 'You're all free to go. I'll expect the universal tomorrow at noon.' He gave them a dismissive nod before disappearing into the kitchen.

'Ivor, have a drink after all your labours!' Col heard Mr Masterson call out heartily.

'Don't mind if I do,' said the Trustee with a note of glee in his voice.

6

Inquest

Dr Brock came to fetch Connie from the cottage the following morning. She was very quiet and did not dare meet his eye as she climbed on the back of the bike, afraid of what she might see.

'All right, Connie?' he asked. His mouth was set in a firm line, quite unlike his normal friendly expression.

'I'm OK,' she said bleakly. There seemed no point telling him that she was worried sick and scared to death. 'What's all this about?'

'Ivor Coddrington wants to see you.'

'Whatever for?' Connie never liked him at the best of times; he was the last person she felt like meeting right now.

'He's been made a Trustee. He's been sent down here to look into what happened last weekend.'

'Oh,' said Connie, fumbling nervously with the strap of her helmet. 'Does he know much about storm-raising then?'

The frown deepened on Dr Brock's face. 'It's not that. I don't know how to say this, Connie, but it's bad. He's investigating you. He's on a witch hunt.'

'Then I'd rather not go,' she said, removing her helmet.

'I'm afraid you've got no choice in the matter, Connie. He has the Society's rules on his side.'

'What can he do—I mean, do to me?'

'I don't know,' Dr Brock said, firing up the engine. 'But I don't expect any of us will like it much, whatever it is.'

Mr Coddrington was holding court in the dining room.

'Bring her in,' he intoned when he learned that Dr Brock and Connie had arrived. Steering Connie by the arm, Dr Brock directed her to a seat on the opposite side of the table from the Trustee. The last time she had met Mr Coddrington he had been all smiles and compliments; today he frowned at her as if she was a particularly stubborn bit of dirt he wanted to rub off the pristine reputation of the Society.

'So, Miss Lionheart, you understand why you have been brought here?'

Connie nodded.

'What was that? I require an answer.' Mr Coddrington's watery eyes blinked at her.

'Yes,' Connie whispered.

'I've heard from the witnesses and I must say that things do not look too good,' Mr Coddrington continued, flipping through his notes. Dr Brock stirred restlessly on her right. Connie looked over anxiously at the papers, wondering what the others had been saying about her. Had even Col not stood up for her? She knew Rat blamed her but she had hoped Col believed her when she said she hadn't really wanted to harm him. 'What have you to say for yourself?'

'I've told Dr Brock already,' she said in a quiet voice.

'But now I want you to tell me,' he said, 'and speak up when you answer me.'

'Ivor!' protested Dr Brock. 'Can't you see how hard this must be for Connie? You're not making it any easier for her talking to her like that.'

'It's not my job to make things easy: it's my job to find out the truth. Go on, Miss Lionheart, answer my question.'

Connie cleared her throat. Given the choice, she would have bolted from the room there and then, but Dr Brock placed a hand on her arm as if he guessed what she was feeling.

'I think I've summoned a storm twice: once last weekend and once in November . . .'

'You think? You mean you might have done it more times?'

Connie was startled by this suggestion. 'I suppose so,' she replied honestly. 'But I've only been aware of two times: once when I sleepwalked—and last weekend.'

'Ah, so you were aware of what you were doing,' he said triumphantly, noting this down.

'No, no, not exactly "aware". I only really knew what I'd done afterwards.'

81

'So you knew what had happened?'

'I sort of did.'

'So you must have been aware of it while you were doing it?'

Connie felt confused. She knew she had watched herself direct the storms, but it had been like being a spectator to a dream. 'It wasn't like that.'

'What was it like? Try and help me understand you here.'

'It was like . . . it was like . . . . ' She faltered.

'You were aware that you had cast a lightning bolt at three Society members?'

'Yes, but I didn't want to hurt them.'

'So you did it against your will?'

'No,' Connie wavered, 'it wasn't like that.'

'So you have already said, Miss Lionheart. Forgive me for not believing you as you are unable to say exactly what it was like. From your own admission, you knew what you were doing. What are we supposed to make of that?'

Connie could feel Dr Brock looking at her. A sob rose in her chest but she was determined not to cry in front of them.

'I don't know,' she said in a strangled voice.

Mr Coddrington got up from his chair and strode to the mantelpiece and flicked some dust off the frame of the Mastersons' wedding portrait.

'Tell me what powers you are calling on, Miss Lionheart.'

'I don't know.'

'You don't know or you don't wish to share your secret with us?' He moved back to the table.

Connie shook her head miserably.

'Answer me!' He leaned forward over her, his face so close that she could scent the faint sour smell of his breath.

'I don't know.'

'Now, come on, Miss Lionheart. You must know that only weather giants have the skill to manipulate the wind and rain as you have done. Which ones are you working with? None of my contacts have channelled their powers through you.'

'I'm not working with anyone!' Connie protested.

'So you're *stealing* power from them, are you? You've found a way of bypassing their consent and thought you'd have some fun? Thought you'd show everyone what the universal could do, did you?'

'Now, Ivor, what's your evidence for that?' Dr Brock exclaimed, looking from Connie to the Trustee.

'I'm sorry to say, Francis,' said Mr Coddrington, smoothing his hair down, his anger scarcely hidden under his formal manner, 'neither Miss Masterson nor I have been able to find any weather giants who have collaborated with the universal in the district. It stands to reason either she is working with renegade forces, such as Kullervo's supporters, with whom we, of course, have no contact, or she has found a way to use their powers without their knowledge. Who knows what a universal can do? Do you?'

'Of course I don't, but it's Connie we're talking about. Look at her! Does she look as if she would do these things? To me, she looks miserable and scared—she's not enjoying her powers in the slightest!'

'Looks can be deceptive, Francis.'

Connie felt the pressure of emotion building inside her as she heard Mr Coddrington's accusations. Had she been doing this? How could she know as she did not understand what was happening to her? What *was* she?

'I think I'm going mad,' she said in a desperate undertone.

'What was that?' Mr Coddrington rounded on her. 'Claiming insanity as your excuse now, are you?'

Connie looked up at him, her eyes stinging with tears. She managed a hopeless shrug.

'Is that your attitude?' he said indignantly. 'Either you are wilfully causing harm to others or you have been driven out of your mind by the powers of the universal: not a very attractive choice of explanations.'

Connie took a deep breath, desperately trying to stop herself breaking down in front of him.

'Mr Coddrington, I really don't know what's happening to me, but I do know I'm a danger. I just want this to stop. I don't want to harm anyone. I don't care what you do, but please help me stop this.'

Dr Brock took a sharp intake of breath, letting her know that he thought this last speech unwise.

'Yes, I'll help you, Miss Lionheart,' said Mr Coddrington, 'I'll help you by suspending you from the Society with effect from today.' He strode to the fireplace to take centre stage to pronounce his judgment. 'You are to have no contact with any members, particularly none of the mythical creatures; you are not to access the universals' reading room again; you are to wait until you are invited to rejoin us once you have proved that you are no longer a danger. That should help you curb that will of yours—or give you time to recover from your insanity, if you prefer. And when you return— if you return—you will restrict your dealings to one companion species only, to be specified by the Trustees. Do I make myself clear?'

Connie sat in stunned silence. Her appeal for assistance had somehow been thrown back at her as suspension. How could she hope to solve this problem on her own?

'Do I make myself clear?'

'Ivor, think what you're doing!' exclaimed Dr Brock, half-rising in his chair.

'I am quite within my powers, Francis,' he replied coolly, still looking at Connie.

'I've no doubt about that, but it's a child in need of our help we're talking about!'

'It's not a child, it's a universal.'

His words pounded into Connie's stupefied brain. 'That's what Kullervo once said,' she whispered.

'In communication with him are you!' Mr Coddrington gloated. 'Oh, it's all coming out now, is it?'

'I am not!' Connie shouted, stung to respond to him. She got unsteadily to her feet as outrage at his unfairness shattered her self-control. 'But you're just like him. You see my gift and you hate me for it! You don't want to help me: you only want to use me or get rid of me!'

'Connie!' Dr Brock said in warning.

'Doing Kullervo's work for him now, are you?' she continued recklessly, her voice cracking. 'I always thought you were on his side. Well, he'll be thrilled to hear what you've done. He's been trying to get me away from the Society for ages and you've done it for him. Congratulations!'

'You heard that, didn't you, Francis: she accused me—a Trustee—of working for Kullervo,' Mr Coddrington said, his voice brittle.

'Yes, but she's upset!'

'I can't let this pass.' Mr Coddrington clasped his hands sanctimoniously in front of him, eyes raised to the heavens. 'I said suspension, but I think I shall make that expulsion. Yes, that's best—best for us all.' He turned to Connie, pale face radiating his righteous anger. 'Your membership of the Society for the Protection of Mythical Creatures is rescinded. You must hand back your badges and have no further communication with any of us. You continue to be bound by your pledge to keep our existence secret.'

'Don't worry: I'm going,' said Connie, thrusting back the chair so that it clattered to the floor. She ripped the badges from her jacket and threw them on the table. 'You know what? The Society's a waste of time, as Kullervo says. I'll be better off without you.' She shook off Dr Brock's arm and ran out of the room.

Bursting from the Mastersons' house, Connie struck out across country back to the cottage. She ran across fields, scrambling over walls, heedless of scrapes and brambles, not bothering to follow

86

any paths. Her body tingled with rage: she could feel it running through her veins to her fingertips. Overhead, clouds began to gather, shifting rapidly, driven by a mounting breeze. In the distance, out to sea, lightning crackled. Connie could feel the dark wave building inside her as all the old reference points of her life collapsed in the earthquake of Mr Coddrington's pronouncement. All she had to do was spread her hands to the sky and she could call this inner turmoil down on the world outside, force it to share her despair—and this time she need not stop. She paused at the edge of the pine plantation, watching the trees creak to and fro under the oppression of the wind, and lifted her hands. Last weekend had proved she could do it: she knew she could summon the storm. She flexed her fingers, poised on the brink of release.

To hell with Mr Coddrington. To hell with the Society.

In the plantation, a tree crashed to the ground, scaring a flock of seagulls into the sky. Their distressed calls echoed off the cliffs jolting Connie back to herself. She had a choice. She would not do it. Whatever she felt, she must not impose her pain on others. She had to resist this urge. Dropping her hands, filled with self-disgust, Connie stumbled back to the cottage and shut herself up in her bedroom.

News that the universal had been expelled by Mr Coddrington travelled round the Society like wildfire. Col couldn't believe it when his grandmother told him what had happened. He immediately abandoned his tea and jumped on his bike to cycle to Rat's house.

Rat was in the garden, playing with his dog, Wolf. Col hovered at the gate.

'Rat, come here.' He lowered his voice, conscious that Connie may be only next door. 'I've got bad news.' He quickly filled him in on Dr Brock's report of the disastrous interview.

'We'd better go see if she's OK,' said Rat, frowning.

Col hesitated. 'Dr Brock said Mr Coddrington has barred anyone from communicating with her.'

'Yeah. But you're not going to take any notice of what that slimeball Coddrington says, are you?' Rat turned to him with genuine amazement. 'Connie's our friend.'

'But I thought you were mad at her for what she did the other week?'

'I was, but she's still my friend. Anyway, sounds as if she had a real go at that Trustee: I want to congratulate her.'

'I hoped you'd say that,' said Col, his face brightening. 'That's what I was thinking.'

The two boys knocked on the back door. It was already getting dark and the lights were blazing in the kitchen. Hugh opened it wearing a striped apron and hands coated in flour, releasing the smell of baking pastry into the night.

'Oh, it's you two, is it? Could you smell the mince pies from next door, eh?'

'Connie in?' asked Col, looking past him and into the kitchen.

'No,' said Hugh, wiping the flour onto his apron. 'She's been off colour today and said she wanted to get a breath of fresh air. She's gone out up to the headland, probably wanting to enjoy it before that wretched farmer spoils it with his wind farm— great ugly thing.' He shook his head sadly. 'But I'm expecting her back any moment now. Do you want to wait inside? Her brother's over for the holidays. He's upstairs playing on the computer. I'm sure he'd like to see you.'

'Thanks, but I think we'll go and look for Connie.'

'All right. I'll have some pies waiting for you when you get back.'

The boys stepped out onto the path.

'Do you think it'll be safe to go up there?' Rat asked, his hands dug deep into his jeans pockets against the cold.

'Yeah,' said Col looking up at the night sky. There were no clouds and the stars were beginning to emerge as the light faded. Only a light breeze was blowing. 'No sign of a storm, is there? I'm sure it'll be OK.'

Connie was sitting on the highest place on the headland looking out to sea. Argand was nestled at her side, keeping her warm with her body, breathing gently on her hands to take away the chill. Argand had sought her out after Connie had hidden in her bedroom. She had scratched at the window and finally extracted a promise that Connie would come out to meet her. The dragonet had threatened to burst into the kitchen when Connie's great-uncle was there if her companion did not agree. Connie leant against

Argand's neck, feeling the warm scales against her cold cheek. She hoped the Society would not punish Argand for meeting her—it did not matter what they did to Connie herself, if indeed there was any more they could do. After all, Argand was only an infant and could not be held responsible for what she did. Companions suffered if they did not see each other. How was the dragonet to understand that there were rules that said she could no longer be with her companion?

The whole situation was hopeless. Perhaps she should run away—go somewhere where she would not be reminded of the Society and all that she was shut off from. But what about her parents in the Philippines, and Uncle Hugh, Evelyn and her friends at home? No, she couldn't do that to them, particularly not when she knew how much they had suffered when she had disappeared for a week last year. But things couldn't go on like this. She'd end up killing someone. Something had to be done about her, but with no help from the Society, and no one else to turn to, she couldn't think what to do. It seemed no one understood her, least of all herself.

Argand snuffed the air and lifted her head on her long neck to look down the track. Connie peered over the top of a clump of brambles and saw Col and Rat climbing quickly towards them.

'I can't meet them. They mustn't see me!' she told Argand as she scrambled to her feet. It was difficult to hide up here; few places offered more shelter than the patch of brambles she had been concealed behind. Intuitively understanding Connie's desire to avoid everyone, Argand launched into the air, leading Connie further west and away from the boys, dancing in front like a golden torch.

Connie heard a shout behind her. They had spotted the light. Panic seized her: she was desperate to disappear.

Argand led Connie down a steep bank into a dry river valley. As she slid down the slope, Connie saw the lop-sided sign warning of deep shafts ahead: they were approaching the old mines, long since abandoned when the seam of tin proved unprofitable. Her great-uncle had forbidden her to go anywhere near the workings but Connie told herself that she would only go as far as the entrance and hide there. No harm could come to her while she was with Argand.

The entrance to the mines yawned ahead—a blacker shape in the gathering gloom. Mr Masterson had fenced it off to stop his sheep or unwary walkers stumbling inside but the barrier was insufficient to stop a determined person from climbing it. Connie struggled over and crouched inside. The only sounds were her own breath, the rustle of Argand's wings against her jeans, and the tinkling of water in the darkness beyond. Just as she thought she had given Rat and Col the slip, she heard someone crashing through the undergrowth, heading in her direction. She crawled in deeper, hoping that they would just look inside and conclude that she had gone another way.

'Connie!' called Col, his voice echoing off the tunnel walls. 'We know you're in there. We want to talk to you.'

Connie crouched as quietly as she could, holding her breath.

'Don't be a prat!' Col shouted again. 'We don't care what Coddrington says: we're going to talk to you if you like it or not!'

Connie heard two thumps as the boys clambered over the barrier. She got to her feet and began to edge a little further in.

'Stay back!' she shouted. 'You mustn't come near me. I'm not safe.'

'Course you're not,' said Rat cheerfully, 'but we can handle that. And the Society can stick their ban!'

'No, no, get back!'

Suddenly, she heard pounding footsteps behind her—a snort of hot breath down her neck—two powerful arms grasped her around the waist. Connie screamed. Argand let out a jet of flame, which reflected off the wet walls in splinters of blinding light. Col gave a shout and Rat stumbled backwards, crashing to the floor. The creature lifted Connie to his shoulder as if she weighed no more than a sheaf of corn and charged off down the tunnel, her screams growing fainter as he galloped sure-footedly away. Argand flew off in pursuit, letting out small blasts of fire at the kidnapper, fearing to unleash her full flame in case she hit Connie.

'What the hell was that?' Rat gasped.

'A minotaur,' Col said, so stunned by what he had just seen that he had not yet moved.

'A what?'

'Bull-headed man. Guardians of labyrinths,

underground mazes.' He shook himself. 'Come on, we've got to go after them.'

'Then we'll need a torch,' said Rat. 'I'll go back and borrow one from home. You stay here in case Argand or Connie return.'

'OK. But hurry!'

Rat vaulted over the barrier, leaving Col alone staring into the dark tunnel down which Connie had disappeared.

7

Minotaur

'Put me down!' Connie shrieked.

'Not until you are safe,' grunted the minotaur. He dodged to the left, avoiding a blast of flame from Argand who was still in pursuit, and squeezed into a narrow passage. Connie heard the dragonet collide with the wall with a sickening thump—her wingspan too broad for this path.

'Argand!' Connie called. The dragonet squealed and hopped a few paces forward but she could not hope to keep up without flight.

Connie bounced painfully up and down on the minotaur's shoulder, her arms dangling, wondering when this nightmare would stop. It was pitch black and she had no idea where he was taking her. Every time he leapt down an unexpected ledge or turned a corner, she was convinced they were going to plunge into one of the old shafts Uncle Hugh had warned her about, but so far the creature had pounded on without a stumble, as if he knew the mines perfectly even in the dark. The creature smelt of sweat and of the dusty old sacking he had fashioned into a tunic for himself. His breath came in hot bursts on her legs. Finally, he seemed to decide they had come far enough. He stopped, lifted Connie from his shoulder and placed her carefully on a pile of old sacks. Afraid to move in the dark with the unseen creature so close, Connie waited.

There was a scrabbling and rasping, then a flash of light as sparks flew up from a flint. With the smell of burning straw strong in the air, the minotaur nurtured a flame in his makeshift hearth and soon had a fierce blaze going. The flickering light shone on the creamy curls of his chest and glanced off the smoother red bristle of his thick-set neck and head. His ears were twitched forward as he bent in concentration over his task. A gold hoop glistened in his wide-set nostrils. Shadows danced on the wall behind him, up to the glittering roof high above, magnifying his curved horns to an immense size. His man's body, flushed red in the firelight, was strongly built, with arms that looked as if they could wrestle any beast into submission.

'I saved you, Universal,' the minotaur said proudly, poking a stick into the fire.

'Saved me?' Connie asked in bewilderment. She had thought it was him she needed saving from.

'You called, so I rescued you,' he said, turning to her to show that one of his large eyes was blinded by a milky white film. The other, dark and sad, looked unflinchingly at her. 'I would not have dared touch you unless you had called. I am not worthy.'

'Not worthy!' exclaimed Connie. 'You've clearly not heard yet. It's me that's not worthy. You're not even supposed to talk to me. The Society's chucked me out.' Unaware of what she was doing, she ripped one of the old fertilizer sacks in her clenched hands as she recalled her expulsion.

'The Society doesn't reach down here,' the minotaur said, not dropping his gaze for an instant. 'This is where the outcast, the sick, the shamed come.'

'Suits me then,' she said, causing the creature to laugh like a pair of wheezy bellows. Her fear of him was rapidly vanishing. 'So why are you here?'

He sat back on his haunches and sighed. 'Wounded in combat. I am no longer fit to fight.' He gestured to his blinded eye. 'We minotaurs guard the world's labyrinths, keeping the secrets of the underworld from the greedy eyes of men. No one would set me to guard anything these days. That's why I've come here—to this blank darkness, one of the many counterfeit labyrinths made by your kind. I'm no longer fit to be anyone's companion.'

His despair and self-hatred was so palpable that Connie could not help herself. She had to comfort him. 'That's not true.' She threw off the sacks covering her legs and reached out to him. He backed away, his skin quivering, his eyes rolling, his good eye showing its white in fear like a beast scenting the slaughterhouse. Determined to prove to this creature that he did not need to shrink from her, Connie took his powerful fist in her hand. Closing her eyes, she sought out his mind, entering the passageways of his thought, calling for him in the torch-lit darkness. She sensed that he was hiding from her, keeping a few steps ahead, leaving only a glimpse of his tail whisking away around a corner or the echo of hooves pounding down distant corridors. She wondered if she should give up; there was no sense in blundering on unwelcome if he did not wish for this encounter.

Just as she was about to release his hand she saw in her mind's eye a shining thread lying on the ground. Stooping to pick it up, she gasped: the thread pulsed in her hand like a heartbeat. Following the trail, Connie made swift progress through the mind-maze, light growing stronger with every step. As she turned the final corner, she stepped out into blazing sunshine which glanced off the hot sand of an arena. The stands were empty, but in the centre a matador and bull were fighting each other—or was it dancing? With light sparkling from his costume, the matador swirled his scarlet cloak over the eyes of the bull as the creature dipped its gilded horns to lunge at the cloth. They whirled and twisted around each other in continual motion, attention only for the other, a dance that united man with bull. Connie sensed the courage in the heart of the minotaur, ready to serve others in the dark places of the earth far from his native element. The fight whirled faster. Wounded by spear and horn, flecks of blood spattered the ground from the bull's scored hide and the matador's gashed side. Connie drank in the bloodlust that rippled in a hot stream through the minotaur's veins, a thirst for death and violence, held only in check by the rules of the dance.

'You have that thirst too, hidden very deep. All humans do,' the minotaur told her. Their encounter had been reciprocal: while she explored his mind, he had been sounding hers.

'I suppose so,' Connie admitted reluctantly, thinking of the storm and the damage some part of her had enjoyed inflicting.

'Yes, but there is more to that than you understand. There is something else lying deep down in the labyrinth of your mind, if you dared to seek it out.'

Connie dropped her hand from his abruptly.

'Let's not go there,' she said.

She opened her eyes to see the creature looking into her face.

'You should not be ashamed of what you are,' he said softly.

'Neither should you.'

He snorted. 'I am no longer fully what I once was. You are still whole.'

'You shouldn't think like that. Your eye—what does it matter?'

'Matter? It is everything—not because of the injury, but because it prevents me from undertaking the tasks I was born to and denies me my birthright.'

It was on Connie's lips to say that she was sure the Society would be able to help him, find him some task that would help him regain his self-respect— then she remembered she was in no position to offer the Society's aid to another.

'So,' she said, changing the subject from these painful thoughts, 'who else is down here besides you?

You said the sick, the injured, and the shamed come here. Who are they?'

The minotaur cast another log on the fire, sending a flurry of sparks up to the ceiling.

'Sick water sprites, homeless wood sprites, fractured rock dwarves—there are many creatures in need of a refuge and they all end up here.'

'Where are they?'

'Waiting for you. They have been waiting for you ever since they learned that you were living nearby. They are waiting for you to make them whole again.'

'But I can't heal them! I told you: I'm not allowed to be a universal any more.'

'You will always be a universal: that is what you are, whether you are in the Society or out of it. You know this in your heart. Did you think I did not see the fear in you? You are afraid to use your powers in case something you cannot control happens again, is that not so?'

Connie nodded, recognizing the truth when she heard it spoken aloud.

'Are you going to let fear of what you might become stop you growing? There are too many stunted lives down here already. We do not need another one to join us.'

As Connie gazed into the shadows at the edge of the pool of light, she noticed for the first time many pairs of eyes blinking back at her. There were hundreds of them—too many for her to distinguish clearly. The minotaur, following her look, spoke to the shadows:

'Come. Show yourselves.'

A trickle of brown water oozed into the light, running to Connie's feet. When it reached her, a form rose out of the pool: a stooped body, emaciated arms and blinded eyes, dressed in weedy rags of rippling cloth. Behind the water sprite, a wood sprite hobbled, its tail a broken stick, its coat bald and the bark skin peeling in raw patches. A third creature stomped into the ring of light, a grey, dully shining rock dwarf with hood thrown back on his shoulders, but his skull was split right across his face, giving his features a distressing lop-sided imbalance, one eye a hand-width higher than the other. Many others followed, all bearing visible signs of injury or sickness until Connie was surrounded by a crowd of beings looking to her with hope gleaming in the depths of their eyes.

'How did they get to be like this?' Connie asked the minotaur, dismayed and shocked by the sight before her.

'It is thanks to what your kind have done, thanks to your pollution, your digging and delving.'

'Like the refinery?' Connie guessed, her heart filling with scalding hatred for Mr Quick and his collaborators.

'Some,' said the minotaur, gesturing to a few creatures huddled at the back. 'But others sickened last year when the farmer here used too much fertilizer on his fields.'

'Mr Masterson?' Connie said incredulously.

The minotaur nodded and pointed with a glowing brand to a group of wood sprites. 'Those were displaced from the hedges when the meadows

100

were ploughed up for the new road; they were driven down here by the machines. None of them can move on and find new homes until you have healed them. That is the task of the universal.'

'But I don't know how!'

'Then you should find out.'

Connie felt the pressure of the many eyes looking to her, believing in her. They did not understand how weak was the person they trusted. 'But I've no access to the Society's library now. How am I going to find out?'

'The answer lies not in books but in yourself if you dare to seek it out. Yet you are too afraid to do so, are you not?'

'Yes,' Connie admitted in a whisper. A disturbed rustle ran through the gathered creatures. A tear fell from the water sprite's unseeing eyes.

'Why has the Society abandoned you all?' she asked desperately. Surely this wasn't for her to solve on her own?

The minotaur grunted. 'The Society has lost its way—it needs a universal at its head again to show it how to care for every creature, especially those of us who have fallen by the wayside.'

'But the Society doesn't want me either, let alone as a leader.'

'Then we too are lost.'

'Connie! Connie!' Voices were calling for her in the distance.

The minotaur rose to his feet and lifted his nose to scent the air. 'They are pursuing you again. Shall I drive them off?'

'No!' Connie got up hastily. 'They're my friends. I was hiding from them because I felt ashamed.'

The minotaur nodded. 'I understand that.'

'I should go back.'

The injured creatures were melting back into the shadows, their passing a whisper of claws and feet on the stone floor.

'Yes, you should,' the minotaur agreed. 'But think about what I have said. We need you. We need you to face your own labyrinth.'

Connie shook her head. 'I'm not ready yet.'

'No, but I will be here to help when you are ready,' he said gently, guiding her to the door of his cave and handing her a burning torch. 'You'll find your friends if you go straight down this passage. Do not go to the left—there is a deep shaft there that even I have never fathomed.'

Connie nodded to show she understood. 'Well, goodbye.' She turned back to him. 'But I don't even know your name.'

'I have no name now,' he said, 'not unless you can find it for me again. Goodbye, Universal.'

'Goodbye,' she said. The door to the cave scraped shut behind her.

8

Pack Leader

Connie woke up on Christmas morning feeling more cheerful than she had since the disastrous interview with Mr Coddrington. She got up and stood for a moment staring at her reflection in the mirror on her dressing table and smiled. A chink of light had appeared in the darkness that had engulfed her since her expulsion. Col and Rat had stood by her—despite all she had done to them. And she had met the minotaur. Although he had alarmed her with his challenge to find out how to help all those creatures, she felt pleased to have a task she could do without the Society's permission—if only she could find the courage for the attempt. With that last thought, she turned her eyes away, no longer liking what she saw there.

Wrapped up in her thickest coat and scarf, Connie slipped her way down the track to the cove. The sea was iron-grey, covered in worried wrinkles under the fretting of the breeze. Seagulls looped overhead. One dropped down to land at her side, a glittering fish in its beak.

'Hello, Mew,' Connie greeted the gull, bobbing a bow in response to hers. 'I see you've had good fishing.'

Mew sliced the frosty air with her call, the fish dropping limp on the stones at her feet. Connie sat on the pebbles beside her, keeping a companionable silence while the bird breakfasted.

'Universal!'

She started. Reverberating up through the soles of her boots was the voice of Gard, the rock dwarf.

'Gard!' she replied in surprise. 'I did not think you'd be able to talk to me again.' She was struck by an unpleasant thought. 'Perhaps you've not heard? I've been expelled.'

'That is why I have sought you out, Universal.'

'But I'm not supposed to talk to anyone in the Society,' she said, feeling it unfair of him to tempt her this way.

'I am too old to care for such things. They can expel me too if they wish—but they will not. Coddrington has made a great mistake with you. The other Trustees will not let the expulsion stand.'

Connie hugged her knees. 'But he said he had the power to do what he liked.'

'He does, but he will be out-voted at the appeal, I am sure of it. All the Trustees will have a voice then.'

A feeling of relief warmed her. Yes, she felt sure Kira Okona, Windfoal, Kinga Potowska, Morjik, Storm-Bird and Eagle-Child would be fair. They would wish to help, not punish.

'The news has reached them thanks to the rock dwarves and they are coming back to England. They will be here very soon. I'll be with you even sooner.'

'Thank you, Gard.'

'Did you really accuse the companion to weather giants of working for Kullervo?' Gard chuckled.

'Er . . . I'm not sure. Possibly. I might've said something like that,' Connie admitted. 'I got a bit carried away.'

'Well, you may have to prepare your apology before they can waive the expulsion. We have to respect our Trustees, even if the person concerned is Ivor Coddrington.'

'OK.' An apology seemed a reasonable price to pay if it meant that she would get help dealing with her problem.

'Keep out of trouble and all should be well. There will be those that oppose your reinstatement, of course: this episode will not have helped dispel the distrust of the universals. It was ever thus.'

'Distrust?'

'Surely you understand by now? Coddrington is motivated by his fear of you, not because he works for our enemy.'

'I see,' Connie said slowly as things began to make sense. 'I cut across the systems, spoil his neat arrangements.'

'That is so. And when you are old enough, and if tradition is followed, you will be invited to lead the Trustees as the representative of the company of the universals. We have not had a leader for many decades for the gift had waned and those who possessed it became too frail. A universal in her prime is what Coddrington fears.'

'Ha!' Connie laughed bitterly. 'I'm no leader, Gard, as you must know. You've seen what lies in me. No one will want me to lead now.'

'I've seen your potential. You are yet a sapling— there are many years before we see the mature tree. You have to keep on growing.'

Connie shivered. 'That was what the minotaur said.'

'Who said?'

'Someone else. Someone wise. I'll tell you when you get here.'

'You are getting chilled, Universal,' Gard noted. 'Your feet are becoming as cold as my stone.'

'You're right.' Connie got up and stamped her feet. 'I'll go in for breakfast now. And thank you, Gard.'

Waving farewell to Mew, Connie ran back to the cottage, her heart now much lighter. She still had friends.

A few hours later, as Uncle Hugh drove Connie and her brother Simon back from church, they came across a man in a long grey coat, striding down the lane to the cottages.

'What on earth can he want?' Hugh wondered aloud. 'Doesn't look the sort to be on visiting terms with the Ratcliffs and I certainly don't know him.'

'Perhaps he's lost?' suggested Simon.

'I don't think he's lost,' said Connie from the back seat. 'I think he's a friend of Rat's.'

As Hugh drew up to his front door, they saw Rat sitting on the wall waiting for his mentor. Connie was eager to get inside before Erik arrived as she did not want to meet a relative of Mr Masterson and another Society member. Rat, however, had spotted her.

'Wait, Connie: you've got to meet Erik.' He grabbed her by the elbow to stop her disappearing.

'I can't,' Connie muttered, trying not to let her brother or Hugh hear. Hugh however had spotted the tussle.

'Course you can—you've plenty of time before lunch,' Hugh announced. 'I'm only just putting the oven on now. Come on, Simon: come and give me a hand.'

'But Connie—' grumbled Simon.

'No "but Connies" thank you. It's Christmas and I've asked *you* to help—not your sister.'

Simon groaned but left Connie and Rat alone without further protest.

'Really, Rat, I shouldn't,' Connie said, pulling away.

By now, the Norwegian had reached them. Connie gave Rat a pained look for having placed her in this awkward situation.

'Erik, this is Connie Lionheart,' Rat said, pushing her forward.

'Nice to meet you—but I think I'd better go now.' Connie could feel herself blushing.

'Why? I have looked forward to meeting you.' Erik shook her hand and didn't let go.

'Well, you see I've been expelled from the Society and you're not really supposed to have anything to do with me.'

'*For noe tull!* Nonsense!' the mentor exclaimed. 'You are a universal—how can we expel you?'

'But Mr Coddrington said that—'

'Mr Coddrington sounds a small-minded bureaucrat, even if my Company did decide to elect him as Trustee. He certainly did not get my vote. As a universal, you are much more than him—you are our pack leader and he is only a whining runt.'

Rat laughed. Connie was both gratified and annoyed with them for making light of the matter. Neither of these frost wolf companions seemed to understand how serious the situation had become.

'Unfortunately, Mr Coddrington has a lot of power now,' she said, meeting Erik's gaze. His eyes had a lupine hunger in their depths; he was not as harmless as he first appeared. Like Rat, there was a toughness to him: hardbitten was the word that came into her mind.

'Perhaps you should show him who is the dominant one in our pack then?' suggested Erik. Reflexively, he touched an old scar on the side of his neck, trophy of some past battle.

'What? Take him on?' Connie shook her head incredulously.

'If necessary.'

'That's not . . . well, just not me.'

Erik continued to gaze at her. 'Maybe you do not know what is you yet. I think you need to meet Icefen. What do you say, Rat?'

Rat nodded eagerly. 'Cool. Can we do it now?'

'I can think of no better time. Rat, you show her how it is done. And, Connie, remember: like it or not, you *are* our pack leader.'

Rat was already dragging on Connie's arm to take her into the cover of the trees at the back of the field. 'Come on, Connie. Let's see if Icefen can carry two.'

That evening, as Connie digested her dinner by the fireside in a sleepy daze, she reflected on what had been her strangest Christmas yet. She and Rat had roamed far and wide on the moor on the back of Icefen, loping across bog, splashing through icy rivers, climbing up hillsides. They had met a number of walkers in their travels, all of whom had scattered before them like frightened sheep. Each time this had happened, Icefen chased them, breathed on them, and the hikers had fallen to the ground unconscious. He seemed to enjoy the game, often inviting the attention of the unwary by flaunting his massive form in the most visible of places. To him, it was a kind of harmless hunting which Rat found hilarious. Connie was not so sure. She wondered what dark dreams would remain with the unfortunate victims exposed to the icy breath.

Hugh and Simon were sitting together on the sofa watching TV.

'Your aunt comes back tomorrow,' Hugh called over to Connie. 'Do you want me to drive you over to Shaker Row to greet her?'

Connie had been wondering what she should do. Before the expulsion, she had been planning to stay on with her great-uncle to give her aunt and Mack some privacy. Now, she thought it better that she got in early with her news before Evelyn heard it from someone else.

'Thanks. I think I'd like to get the house ready for them.'

'That will suit me. Simon and I are off to the match in Chartmouth. You don't want to come with us, I suppose?'

'How did you guess?'

'Oh, it's just the way you roll your eyes every time Uncle Hugh and I talk about football,' commented Simon sourly.

'Each to his own, Simon,' said Hugh. 'I've noticed you groaning every time Connie says something about her society. Are you going to any more meetings, love?' he asked Connie. 'I've not noticed you heading off for your usual activities the last few days.'

'No, I'm having a break.'

'Packed up for Christmas, have they?'

'Something like that.'

'That's a shame. I know how much you enjoy them.'

On Boxing Day, Hugh and Simon dropped Connie outside Number Five and headed for the twelve o'clock kick-off in Chartmouth. She watched them go as Madame Cresson, her aunt's cat, wound happily around her ankles.

'Has Mrs Lucas been looking after you all right?' Connie asked, bending down to fondle the cat's thick ginger fur. Madame Cresson looked up at her with her golden eyes and blinked, as if to say that she had deigned to accept the neighbour's ministrations but only on sufferance. 'Well, Evelyn will be back soon. You'll not have to put up with it any longer.'

Letting herself in through the back door, Connie found the house unpleasantly cold and unwelcoming, despite the fact that it had only been empty for two weeks. The heating had been ticking over on the minimum required to stop the pipes freezing and there was a definite chill in the air. Deciding her first task must be to warm the place up, Connie went through the house turning on heaters and switching up the boiler. The last room she entered was the front room, a place she rarely chose to go as it always had a mournful feel that she associated with the terrible night she had woken on the beach. Connie switched on the old electric fire with a clunk and wrinkled her nose at the smell of singeing dust. Thinking she had better wait to check nothing caught fire, she sat on the unyielding sofa. As ever, her eyes were attracted to the mantelpiece. Why was there a statue of a white horse and a figurine of a bronze bear up there? She had never asked her aunt but, wondering about it now, the answer seemed obvious: they must have been the companion species of her great-aunt and her husband, both of whom had been Society members. But which was which, she wondered?

The roar of a motorbike in the lane outside disturbed her from these thoughts. Evelyn and

Mack were here already and she felt nowhere near prepared for what would be a difficult conversation. Dashing back to the kitchen, Connie arranged the holly spray she had brought with her in the centre of the table, filled the kettle, and switched it on, attempting to make everything seem as normal as possible. Footsteps crunched up the path and she heard voices at the back door. Connie took a deep breath, hitched a smile onto her face and waited for them to enter.

Evelyn Lionheart breezed into the kitchen looking tanned and happy. Dumping her bags by the door, she folded her niece in a hug.

'Connie—it's so nice you're here!' she said, kissing her on the cheek.

Mack came in carrying a light rucksack, throwing it on top of Evelyn's luggage.

'Everything all right?' he asked. 'How's that son of mine?'

'He's OK, Mr Clamworthy,' Connie said awkwardly.

'Mack, darling. You make me feel a hundred calling me Mr Clamworthy all the time. Anyway, now I'm your—what is it?—uncle, I suppose. No way am I going to allow you to call me "Uncle", so it'll have to be Mack.'

The more he said, the more Connie wondered how she was going to broach the subject of what had happened in their absence. She decided she would wait till they were all sitting down.

'Would you like a cup of tea or coffee?' Connie asked. 'Oh no, I've forgotten to get in any milk.'

'Don't worry, black coffee for both of us will be fine,' said Evelyn, rummaging in her bag. 'Look, I got this for you.' She held out a kikoi, a brightly coloured length of cloth like the one that Kira Okona, the unicorn companion, wore. 'You can go into competition with Kira at the next meeting with the Trustees.'

'Yeah,' said Connie in a hollow voice, scrunching the material up in her hands. 'Thanks—it's lovely.'

Pouring the hot water onto the coffee grounds, she let Evelyn and Mack chatter on about their honeymoon. Mack appeared to be turning over a new leaf: he had not left his bride once to go swimming with the Kraken.

'Well, I thought "no banshees on Zanzibar, mate" so it wouldn't be fair,' he said with an uncharacteristically virtuous look.

'Fraud!' hit back Evelyn. 'The Kraken doesn't even like the shallow waters around Zanzibar—it was nowhere near us!'

'Well, you've got me there, I must admit,' said Mack with a laugh.

Connie saw that they had already fallen into the good-humoured mocking of people at ease with each other. Despite her misgivings about Mack as an uncle, it looked as if all was going well—so far. She placed the coffee down in front of them and sat at the table.

'So,' said Evelyn at last, 'how are things with you? Training going OK?'

Connie cleared her throat. 'Er . . . I've got some bad news.'

'My mother's all right, isn't she?' asked Mack, putting his cup down.

'She's fine.'

'The wind farm didn't get turned down, did it?' asked Evelyn.

'No. Sorry, I should've mentioned: Rat told me that got the go-ahead last week.'

'That's great. So, what's up?' Evelyn said, shaking her head as if she could not imagine anything else could possibly be wrong.

'I don't know how to tell you, so I'd better just say it. You'll hear soon enough anyway. I've been expelled from the Society.'

'Expelled!' Evelyn put her cup down abruptly, spilling steaming black liquid all over the table.

'You're joking, right?' said Mack, wiping his mouth on the back of his hand.

'No, I'm not.' Connie got up to fetch a cloth to clear away the mess.

'Leave it,' said Evelyn tersely. 'You had better tell us the whole story.'

Connie would have preferred to have fiddled around with the cloth so she could avoid her aunt's eye but Evelyn insisted that she sit still and recount every detail. She was surprised: Evelyn seemed more worried to hear about the storm-raising than the interview with Mr Coddrington.

'You say you've done this twice now, Connie? Why ever didn't you tell me?' Evelyn looked appalled.

Connie shrugged. 'I was afraid—ashamed, I s'pose.'

'And what does Dr Brock say about it?'

'It was his idea to go to the Trustees for help. That's how Mr Coddrington got involved.'

Evelyn sat in silence for a moment, looking at her niece intently. Connie's insides were squirming: she felt sure that she was about to be scolded again.

'Well, I think it's outrageous!' Evelyn said finally. 'You're in deep trouble—and what does the Society do? Throw you out! As if that is going to solve anything!'

Connie looked up. This was not the reaction she had been expecting. She had thought her aunt would be cross with her for concealing her storm-raising, cross because she had shouted at the Trustee, cross because she had been expelled.

'Coddrington's an idiot,' Mack interjected.

'He's thrown you out at the very time you most need us. Well, we're not going to take any notice of that, are we? And anyone in the local Society who thinks differently will have me to reckon with!'

'There's an appeal. Gard thinks I'll be all right,' Connie said. She felt much better already, knowing that Evelyn was firmly on her side. She should have told her long ago.

There was a gentle tap on the back door. Evelyn got up to open it and found Dr Brock on the doorstep, bearing a box of groceries.

'Evelyn, good to see you back!' he said, kissing her lightly on the cheek. 'Had a good holiday?'

Evelyn nodded. 'Come in.'

Dr Brock entered the kitchen and spotted Connie sitting at the table.

'Ah. So you've heard then? I came over to tell you before you got a garbled version from someone else, but I'm glad you got to hear it first from Connie. We're appealing against the decision, of course.'

Evelyn stood with her back to the kitchen sink.

'Stuff the appeal! We can't wait for the Society to get its act together. Connie needs help and she needs it now. If the Chartmouth Chapter can't help one of its own, then what are we here for?'

'But, Evelyn, Connie's long-term interests lie in getting back in the Society, you must see that.'

'As far as I'm concerned, she still is *in* the Society and I intend to treat her as such. Anyone who disagrees with me had better keep out of my way.'

Dr Brock put the groceries on the table and sat down, toying with his dragon-skin gloves.

'Look, you don't know what it was like. Connie, for whatever reason, almost blasted Col, Rat, and me off the face of the earth. People are understandably upset. She's dangerous.' He turned to Connie. 'Sorry, Connie, but it's true.'

'I know,' Connie replied, looking down at her hands.

'Well, if you put it like that, we're all dangerous,' said Evelyn. 'The Kraken's not exactly a laugh a minute; my banshees wouldn't be invited into polite company; and as for your dragons, they don't make very good houseguests, do they?'

'Of course not,' Dr Brock sighed. 'But they have their actions under control.'

'Well, I don't know . . .' interjected Mack.

'You don't agree with Coddrington, do you, Francis?' asked Evelyn.

'Of course not, though I can understand his position. Connie did accuse him of working for Kullervo.'

'Good for you, girl!' said Mack.

Evelyn brushed this aside. 'You can tell the others that as far as Number Five Shaker Row is concerned, Connie is still a member of the Society. If anyone wants to come here, they'd better be of that opinion too—or else they should keep away.'

'I agree with you, of course, Evelyn, but there is a virtue in keeping a cool head on these matters for a few weeks. We do not want to hand Ivor Coddrington more proof to back up his decision. Connie flouting his ruling would be just the kind of thing he will seize on and use against her.'

Evelyn was a little deflated by this view of the situation. 'She lives here, doesn't she? He can't object to that?'

Dr Brock got up. 'He would if he could, but, no, I don't think he can take issue with that.' He strode over to the door. 'Well, goodbye to you all—and Merry Christmas.' He let himself out, closing the door with a firm click behind him.

'Well now,' said Evelyn, rounding on Connie, 'what are we going to do about your sleepwalking?'

'Lock her in her room?' suggested Mack.

'I don't think that'll do any good,' said Connie. 'The sleepwalking me would find a way out, I'm sure of it.'

'Yes, and I don't want you climbing out of your window in the middle of the night,' said Evelyn.

An idea came to Connie. 'Can I have Argand to stay?'

Evelyn was taken aback. 'I thought you heard what I just said about dragons as houseguests. Anyway, what's this to do with your sleepwalking?'

'What stopped me last time was an encounter with Argand. If she was close by, she could snap me out of it before I did any damage—bring me back to myself.'

Evelyn smiled with relief to hear so simple a solution. 'In that case, of course.'

'A dragon sleepover. Better invest in a fire extinguisher, Evie,' said Mack, putting his feet up on the table.

9
Sentinel

'I'm not sure you should come, dear,' said Mrs Clamworthy to Col as she buttoned her coat. 'It's all very well for old folk like me to ignore the ban, but I don't want you to put your training at risk.'

'Don't be daft, Gran; of course, I'm coming,' Col replied. He was already in his jacket and waiting for his grandmother by the back door. 'What kind of friend would I be to Connie if I didn't?'

Mrs Clamworthy sighed. It was the last day of the Christmas holidays and Evelyn had called a meeting of what she termed 'the pro-Connie faction' of the Chartmouth Chapter. Purpose of the meeting: to see if by pooling their wisdom they could discover a way to help Connie solve her problem.

Col was pleased to find that there was a good turnout at Number Five by the time he and his grandmother arrived. He hoped Connie would take heart from this show of support for her. Mack and Evelyn were there, of course, sitting at either end of the table. Connie had taken a seat in a corner, as if she was not sure if she should be taking part. Argand was stretched out at her feet asleep, twitching in her dreams. Col knew Connie well enough to realize that she would be worrying about what would happen to her supporters if the Society found out they were holding this meeting but she avoided his eye when he tried to give her a reassuring smile.

Rat was perched on the draining board, playing with one of Evelyn's mobiles that twirled above the sink, jiggling it so violently that it looked in imminent danger of collapse. Seated by Evelyn were Jessica Moss and her selkie companion, Arran, for the moment in his human shape. To Col's eyes, Arran always had the look of a seal about him with his large soulful dark eyes, long paddle-shaped hands, thick brown hair that shone still wet from a swim. Jessica's expression was defiant as if she dared anyone to question her right to be there. Arran by contrast looked at ease, the threat of penalties for consorting with Connie was so much water off his smooth back.

Dr Brock sat opposite Arran, calmly reading through some correspondence. Erik Ulvsen was chatting to Mack—they seemed to be well on the way to making friends. By Erik's side was a frequent visitor from the London branch: Horace Little, also a companion to selkies. Horace, with old-fashioned gallantry, leapt to his feet to offer Mrs Clamworthy his seat.

'Now, I think that's everyone,' said Evelyn, calling them to order. 'Thank you all for coming. We know what you're risking in showing your support for Connie in this way.'

The room went quiet. Col saw that Connie now had her head in her hands.

'I didn't call this meeting to annoy Headquarters . . .'

'Didn't you, Evie?' interrupted Mack with a grin. 'That's not what you said last night.'

'OK, I didn't call this meeting *only* to annoy Headquarters,' Evelyn conceded. Col smiled: he knew that his father welcomed any opportunity to annoy the Society authorities; this same attitude had obviously spread to his new wife. 'I called it because I think that we can best help Connie if we put our heads together and see if we can cast some light on what's gone wrong with her gift.'

'Hmm,' said Horace. 'I wish we had a unicorn companion among us—or even a rock dwarf companion—someone used to healing or exploring the layers of the mind.'

'So do I,' agreed Evelyn. 'But as the Society authorities in their wisdom have seen fit to cast Connie off, we're all we've got, so we'll have to do.'

At that moment, there was a knock at the back door. Connie shrank into the shadows. Dr Brock and Horace exchanged a worried look, wondering if the secret of their meeting had already been betrayed. Erik and Mack stood up, ready to defend Connie from any incomers. Rat was the only one present who seemed completely unconcerned. He jumped down from the sink and flung open the door.

'What d'you want?' he challenged the figure standing in the dark. The light from the kitchen did not seem to have any impact on the stranger. They could make nothing of the black shape amongst the shadows.

'I want to come in, young man,' came the reply.

'Not before you tell us who you are, mate,' Rat said, not moving aside.

'I'm Gard, a rock dwarf.' The visitor cast back his hood, revealing a coal-black craggy face that gleamed in the lamplight. 'I have come a long way and I'm used to a warmer welcome than this at this house.'

'Hey, a rock dwarf: that's cool! You can come in,' said Rat, staring fascinated at Gard.

Dr Brock and Horace rose to their feet to welcome their old friend. Even Connie left her corner to greet him. Gard took both Connie's hands in his black fists.

'I told you I would come.'

She smiled back at him, her thanks unspoken but understood. Gard swung round to face the Society members.

'And what is all this I see? An illicit meeting?' he asked sternly.

'Yes,' said Evelyn, her head held high.

'Good, good!' said Gard, his voice relaxing into a chuckle. 'I thought Connie was in need of a friend, but I find her surrounded by them: that is excellent.'

'We were just saying, Gard,' said Dr Brock, offering the rock dwarf a chair which he refused, 'that we need someone experienced in plumbing the depths of the mind. Your arrival could not have been more timely. Perhaps you will be able to find the answer for us.'

Gard stood by the fireplace, feet planted on the hearthrug, his mallet swinging loosely in his right hand. His dark eyes, almost hidden in his coal-black face but for a gleam in their depths, scrutinized them all carefully.

'You look to me for answers, you say?' he said gruffly. 'Have you been able to find the question then?'

'The question?' asked Dr Brock.

'Yes. I think we do not really know what we are asking ourselves. Have we decided whether we want to know why Connie is doing this, or who is doing this through Connie? They are very different matters. Some of you, I know, still believe it is Connie who is doing these things. Perhaps even in part of her mind, Connie thinks that too, or why else would she be hiding from you, her friends?'

The eyes of the company turned to Connie. He was right: she had again slid back into her corner.

'It seems to me that her fear of herself is our main problem. Until she embraces what it is to be a universal—the dark as well as the light—she will not understand what is happening to her. And if she has the courage to do this, we must also have the fortitude to accept what she becomes. There should be no part of her, no matter how terrible, that we should shrink from.'

Col looked over at Connie. Was he ready to accept her with all her powers even if they were as fearsome as Gard hinted? He had almost lost his life the other week trying to help her. Now that he knew such things lay within her, would he be willing to do so again? He hoped he would but he had to be honest that his feelings for her were now mixed with fear.

'You make it sound as if you're asking us to take a terrible risk,' said Mrs Clamworthy in a quavering voice.

Gard looked hard at her. 'I am. You did not think your support for the universal was simply a matter of siding against Ivor Coddrington, did you? Supporting her is consenting to share the risk of exploring what it means to be a universal. She has been left too much on her own over these last two years. The Society has neglected its greatest treasure. Each of you have, or had, mentors to guide you. Who has been doing that for Connie?'

'We've tried,' said Evelyn, 'but none of us are universals: we don't understand what it is like to be one—*how* to be one.'

'Well, it seems to me that you are finding out now the hard way. Being a universal has always been perilous.'

'So, what do you think we should do, Gard?' asked Dr Brock.

'Our task is not to find the answer, but to help the universal to find it for herself. Accompany her on this journey and not blame her for the consequences. She must feel no shame in what she discovers. I do not know what that will be: it might be that she is wilfully using the storms to harm others then lying to herself—and us—about it afterwards—that is very possible. The human minds I have known are quite capable of such self-deception. It may also prove that other powers are at work. What they might be, I do not know yet.'

Col was feeling uncomfortable. Gard was discussing Connie almost as if she was not there. Surely her voice should be heard? Was any of this making sense to her?

'Are you always so gloomy?' Rat broke in from the far end of the kitchen. 'We all know she's a menace, but then my ma thinks I'm a menace. And what's life without a little bit of risk, I ask you? I'm right behind Connie. In fact, I was hoping you'll let me come along for the ride. It's not every day your friend turns out to have cosmic powers now, is it?'

Gard's stern face cracked into a smile.

'I've not yet met you properly, young man, but I like your attitude. You must have some iron in your bones. What is your companion species?'

'The frost wolf.'

'Ah,' Gard said with a knowing look, 'that explains it.'

'I'm with Rat,' Col spoke up. 'Connie's all right by me—all of her. I'll just have to add some new moves to my training to dodge any more lightning bolts that come in my direction.'

'I never thought that unreasonable of her,' added Mack with a wink at his son, 'you often drive me crazy too. A lightning bolt was probably what you deserved.'

The atmosphere was visibly lightening as one by one each member spoke out to confirm their acceptance of the danger they were all running in backing Connie. The only person from whom they had not yet heard was Connie herself. Gard turned to her.

'You see you have some faithful friends, Universal. Are you going to let us help you find the answer to your own mystery?'

Connie was struggling with conflicting feelings. Of course, she was grateful that they were all coming out on her side and that they had declared that they would accept her, all of her, no matter what that meant. On the other hand, she did not want to put them in danger—none of them understood what they were letting themselves in for. She could not drag them into her trouble. They had already put their membership of the Society on the line for her sake; she did not want to ask them for any more. Nor did she want to expose herself to them. She hunched her shoulders and stared at her hands, which were clenched on her knees, and refused to look up.

'She's being a prat again,' said Rat cheerfully. 'You can tell when Connie wants to hide from us all—she goes into this silent misery act.'

'Ssh!' said Mrs Clamworthy.

'Yeah, Rat, not everyone has the sensitivity of a stone like you do,' said Col.

'I could take exception to that remark, Col Clamworthy,' said Gard, but he was smiling. 'I would not have phrased it in quite the way our young friend did, but it is time the universal stopped shutting herself off from us all—that was always the abiding sin of the company of universals and lies at the root of many of the failings of the Society. She should remember that, though her gift is special, it is only an extension of the gift that we all have. All of us have to learn that we contain the ugly as well as the beautiful.'

Gard's words took Col back to his experience the previous year as Kullervo's companion. He realized that he could help her because he had had to face something similar himself.

'Look, Connie,' Col said, his face reddening as he spoke up before the company. He had kept this experience to himself and had not intended to share it with others. 'I caused suffering too last year—you saved me from it so you know what I'm talking about. You know something of what I became then.' He took a breath. 'I discovered then, as Kullervo had made me into a warrior, that part of me—a part that I wish didn't exist—well, it liked spilling blood and causing suffering.' The room was silent, but Col somehow found the nerve to continue. 'I've had to accept that this urge will always be with me. It has to be mastered so that I control it rather than let it control me.' He got up and went to sit on the arm of her chair. 'You've got to stop thinking you're especially bad, or especially dangerous. You must let us help you as you once helped me.'

Connie looked up and met Col's eyes. She remembered the cold youth Colin who had taken his place and the frightened child Col she had rescued from Kullervo's assault. He had been brave to admit this secret about himself; she had to find similar courage.

'OK, OK,' she said shakily, 'I give in. You all accept me as I am. I just hope you know what you're doing.'

Evelyn pulled Connie out from her corner.

'Come on,' said Evelyn, 'no more hiding in the shadows: we've got work to do. Where shall we start?' She looked at Gard expectantly.

'I think I know,' admitted Connie. 'I think I need to take Gard to the underworld.'

A few days later, a small party of Society members headed for the mines. Gard refused to ride in Dr Brock's sidecar, saying that being so close to the ground made him feel ill; his bond with the earth rushed by so fast it made his head spin. Connie had drawn the short straw and thus had a worm's eye view of Gard clinging to the doctor's waist, his head hidden in a spare helmet, his craggy extremities disguised in leather boots and gloves. Mack and Col rode the second bike, having volunteered to head off any inquisitive approaches.

'Where's Rat?' Connie asked as they slowed down for the bumpy track to the cottages. 'I thought he wanted to come along?'

'He did,' replied Dr Brock, 'but I persuaded him his time would be better spent keeping his family out of the way. Now your brother's back at school there should be no one about because Horace has taken Hugh out on a trip in their boat.'

'So why do Mack and Col have to be here?'

'Just in case.'

Dr Brock's caution turned out to be farsighted. It was not Hugh or the Ratcliffs that proved to be the problem. When the bikes pulled up outside the cottages they discovered the lane full of construction vehicles.

Mack removed his helmet and whistled. 'Phew—I didn't know about this. Then again, Evie and Masterson aren't talking, thanks to our little storm-raiser, so I s'pose he's gone full steam ahead and started building the wind farm without telling us. Doesn't waste time, does he?'

Builders were swarming over the hillside; trucks bounced across the fields with loads of earth; like badgers on a sandy bank, JCBs had made a good start on digging foundations.

'How are we going to get Gard over to the mines with no one noticing?' asked Col. 'Do you think we should come back this evening?'

'It will be fine,' said Gard, stamping his feet, relieved to be back on solid ground. 'If you gather around me, no one will see. I'll keep my hood up, boots and gloves on.'

Connie led them to the footpath across the edge of the field. There were fewer builders this way, though there was a small gathering of men by the fence, all looking at a large plan that was flapping about in the wind. Connie hoped they would be too interested in their discussion to notice the strange party of walkers.

As they approached, the nearest man turned round. It was Mr Masterson. His eyes fell on Connie at the front of the group and his normally affable face hardened. Muttering something to the builders, he sent them up the field and stood waiting for her to draw level with him. Connie wondered what she should do. She could hardly turn and run, but neither could she pretend she was only out for an innocent stroll, not with Gard with them.

'Miss Lionheart,' Mr Masterson said, 'what are you doing on my land?'

'I thought it was a public footpath,' she replied meekly, not wanting to provoke him further.

'It is. But I would've thought that you at least would not have the audacity to revisit the scene of your crimes.' Mr Masterson now took in the rest of her party. 'And with the very people you almost killed. Very odd indeed!'

'Have you a problem with us being here, Masterson?' asked Mack, the edge of a threat in his voice.

'But she's banned! None of you are supposed to be with her!'

Mack took a step forward to lay his hand on Connie's shoulder, revealing Gard behind him.

'And with a rock dwarf—in broad daylight!' Mr Masterson's eyes bulged apoplectically as he cast a frantic look back up the field to where his construction team were working.

'Then you had better let us pass, Clive,' said Dr Brock reasonably, 'before someone notices us.'

Mr Masterson struggled with his conflicting desire to turn them back, which was likely to create more of a disturbance with Mack there, or let them pass.

'Look, Francis, you know I have nothing personal against the girl, but I'm a loyal member of the Society, you should not be associating with her like this,' he appealed to Dr Brock. 'You are putting me in an impossible situation.'

'You must do as you see fit,' said Gard gruffly. 'Let others do what they see fit.'

'All right, but on your own heads be it,' Mr Masterson said, turning his back on them and striding away. 'I'll have nothing more to do with the lot of you if you've chosen her side.'

Col felt deeply sorry for Connie as the party moved off again. She did not have the nature of someone like Rat who would laugh off such comment. He moved up the line to walk beside her and pretended not to notice as she hurriedly wiped her eyes.

'He's always been an idiot, Connie,' he said, 'you mustn't take any notice of him.'

'Of course I don't,' Connie said in a too hearty voice. 'I was just worried about what he might do to the rest of you.'

Col shrugged. 'Who cares? We know what we've let ourselves in for.'

Col and Connie led the way down the valley to the entrance to the mines. Recent rain had brought the streambed to life and a gush of water now issued from the mouth of the tunnel. The place had a dank and gloomy feel, smelling of damp stone and rotting leaf mould. Connie peered into the entrance as Dr Brock shone a torch over her shoulder. Its light glanced off the constant ooze of water that made the green-stained walls slick to the touch.

'I suppose we had better try and find the minotaur,' suggested Dr Brock. 'Can you remember the way?'

Connie shook her head. 'Not without Argand. Can you, Col?'

'Er . . . I think we went straight, then a bit to the right.' He sighed. 'No, I can't, to tell you the truth.'

'I'll try and summon him then,' said Connie, 'but I'd better go in alone. Knowing the minotaur, he would probably charge first and ask questions later.'

Connie took a few steps inside to the point where the minotaur had seized her on Christmas Eve. The steady 'plunk, plunk' of a drip measured the moments as she dipped into her mind to call him, seeking out the golden thread of his presence. At first he eluded her—his thoughts absorbed in the disturbance of the ground over his head where the builders were working, but finally he caught her voice amid the noise.

'Universal, you have returned,' he said joyfully. 'I will come to you.'

Connie sat and waited, counting the drops as they fell from ceiling to floor. A snort behind her and she felt the warm touch of the minotaur on her shoulder.

'I knew you would come back,' he said, 'the others will be pleased. Come.'

Connie placed a hand on his powerful arm. 'Wait. I have some friends with me—people I want you to meet.'

The minotaur backed away, looking over her head in alarm, two grey plumes of breath from his nostrils visible in the faint light.

'I do not wish to see others.'

'You sound like I did,' said Connie wryly.

'What did you say?'

'You mustn't be afraid. They're here to help me. They're my friends.'

The minotaur pawed the ground with his right foot, poised between fight and flight.

'Please,' she begged, 'meet them for my sake?'

He bowed his great head. 'For your sake.'

Connie turned back to the entrance. She could see the silhouettes of the others, anxiously trying to make out what she was doing in there.

'You can come in,' she called. 'He's agreed to see you.'

Dr Brock switched on the flashlight. The beam danced into Connie's eyes and startled the minotaur. He grunted in distress.

'Turn it off!' Connie called. 'It's too bright. You'll have to find your way without it.'

'How are we to do that?' asked Mack as they moved into the tunnel.

'I need no lamps; I see very well in the dark,' said Gard, striding resolutely forward.

'That's all very well for you,' murmured Mack, 'but what about us mere mortals?'

'I will lead you,' growled the minotaur, standing with his arms crossed.

'Look,' said Connie. 'I'll hold onto our guide; you hold onto each other and Col can hold onto me. No problem.'

'No problem?' muttered Mack to Col. 'A bull-headed monster is leading us in the dark to his lair, and she says "no problem".'

'Shut up, Dad!' whispered Col. 'He's her friend—not a monster.'

'Hah! You've obviously not heard the stories I've heard about minotaurs: they rip apart anyone who stumbles upon their secrets.'

'And you, human . . .' (Col and his father both jumped) ' . . . have not heard the story about our sharp senses!' bellowed the minotaur. 'We can hear the fall of a water droplet in a cavern a mile deep.'

'Er . . . no, I hadn't heard that one. And I'm not interested in any of your secrets, mate . . . er . . . Mr Minotaur. Let's just get that straight.'

Mack moved further off, as the minotaur stared suspiciously after him, fists flexing.

'Hadn't we better go?' whispered Connie, touching the creature on his forearm.

He grunted his agreement and took her hand in his.

The line of walkers set off. Gard walked by Connie's shoulder, tapping the walls of the tunnel thoughtfully, listening to the echoes. Col, Dr Brock, with Mack bringing up the rear, trudged behind; they had to take on trust that Connie would not let them be led astray, or into one of the many shafts that lay hidden in the shadows. After ten minutes of walking, they arrived at the minotaur's cave where he had a fire already burning. In the light, his good eye inspected each guest, lingering longest on the rock dwarf. Col returned the scrutiny, amazed by the beast that stood before him—a strange marriage of man and bull: neck the width of a buffalo's, arms that would to put any Olympic weightlifter to shame.

'Why did you bring them here, Universal?' the minotaur said in a tender voice to Connie.

'When I came here the first time, you said that you could help me find the way through the labyrinth of my mind,' she replied. 'My friends have come to help. Gard here knows the layers of the mind better than anyone. Dr Brock—he's a dragon companion and can read dreams. The others are here because they're my friends.'

The minotaur crouched down on his haunches in front of her. 'I do not take others into the mazes. I can guide only those with whom I have a bond.'

'But you can, you see,' said Connie eagerly, sitting forward. 'I can hold many voices of mythical creatures in my mind at once—that's the chief gift of the universal. And through their bond with their companion species, my human friends can be there too.'

'Hmm,' grunted the minotaur, looking at her sceptically. 'You think this will work?'

'I've done it before.'

Gard stepped forward, his dark skin glittering jewel-like in the wavering light. His stout form was level with the minotaur's head as that creature brooded by the fire.

'I need you to guide me, Minotaur. I can pass through the layers of my companion's mind, but only those she is willing to show. Something is hiding inside the universal, something we must pursue and reveal to the light. We need a skilled person to lead us and, without you, we are unlikely to succeed. I think it is a task that has been appointed for you.'

135

On those words, the minotaur's ears pricked forward, his face alert as if snuffing the scent of battle. 'My task, you say, Rock Dwarf?'

Gard nodded. 'This is a task that needs an inner eye and does not depend on outward sight. You are the perfect guide. You are the one who should guard the universal's labyrinth.'

Silence fell.

Finally, the minotaur spoke: 'Then I agree.'

He startled them all by raising his head to the ceiling and giving out a great bellow—a battle cry and a shout of joy. Col thought for one terrified moment that the minotaur was about to turn and gore them all with his horns, but saw instead that he had grasped Connie and folded her in an embrace. 'You have restored me to myself. I said you would.'

Connie laughed, wiping away tears. 'So have you found your name again?'

'Yes,' he cried. 'The Universal's Sentinel! I'll be the envy of all my kind when they hear of my new title.'

'Well, Sentinel,' said Gard. 'Shall we begin?'

10

Cave Paintings

Gard beckoned the minotaur to take a place at Connie's side. Sentinel sat with his arm around her, good eye roving the shadows, alert for any threat to his charge.

'It will be very dangerous to enter the mind of the universal. How shall we undertake this journey?' asked Dr Brock, stirring the embers to send sparks whirling to the ceiling.

'Our numbers should be few,' said the minotaur.

'I will come, of course,' said Gard, 'and Dr Brock should accompany us.'

'That means we need Argot,' said Dr Brock. 'I will have to summon him before I can join the shared bond.'

'What about one of Connie's guardians—surely either Evelyn or Mack should be with us?' suggested Gard.

Connie felt uneasy. She had not liked her encounter with the Kraken nor the banshees.

'I'll come,' volunteered Mack quickly.

'Hang on a minute, Dad, just how are you going to get the Kraken here?' said Col, reading Connie's dismayed expression.

'Col's right,' said Connie, trying not to offend Mack. 'And I think that both the banshees and the Kraken are too unpredictable to be part of this.'

'So that rules us out,' said Mack, a shade grumpily.

'But not Col,' suggested Dr Brock. 'As, dare I say it, one of your closest friends, someone who knows you better than any of us, I think he can be helpful.'

'Yeah, Connie.' Col grinned at her. 'After all, you trampled through my mind last year. About time I got to pay a return visit. You won't mind us, will you, Connie?'

'No, I think I can cope with you and Skylark,' she said. 'If you're sure you want to do this.'

Col squeezed her hand. 'I'm sure.'

There was no prospect of bringing Argot and Skylark to the mine until nightfall so the party dispersed: Mack to inform Evelyn of what was happening, Dr Brock and Col to fetch their companions. Connie and Gard remained behind with the minotaur.

Connie sat for a long time watching the light flickering on the walls and ceilings, the horns of the minotaur interlocking in mock shadow-battle with the shovel-shaped head of the rock dwarf.

Connie was the first to break the silence. 'There are many other creatures down here, Gard. Hurt creatures. I'd like to help them.'

Gard poked the fire with a stick. 'There are many such colonies in the secret places of the earth,' he said. 'All are waiting for healing but the Society has been at a loss what to do for them. I fear we have become too preoccupied by other matters—Kullervo not the least of them. If you can heal these creatures, then you have a great task ahead of you, Universal, perhaps one that will require more than a single person's lifetime, so brief is your stay on earth.'

He fell silent. Connie guessed that he was still mourning for Frederick Cony. It must be hard for a deathless creature to see his friends pass away again and again. Never to die: it was hard to imagine a life like that.

'Gard, you're immortal, aren't you? What was it like at the beginning of everything?' she asked.

Gard looked up. 'The beginning? I am immortal as long as this world endures, but even I was not there at the beginning. Then we were all stardust, sent into space by our Creator.'

'Our Creator?'

'Do you think we sprang from nothing? I believe we are part of a greater design—something that is more than the sum of atoms that makes up our being. Each life has value and meaning—even the briefest.'

The minotaur grunted. 'The world I know is not like that,' he said. 'It's full of pain and grief, short bitter lives and desperate ends. Where is your Creator in all this?'

'My friend, you said yourself but a short while ago that the universal had restored you. Through her,

139

through the hands of others, we can see our Creator at work. I believe that we each have the power to heal and make whole if only we can find it. There is hope for the creatures hiding here if the universal can rise to the challenge.'

Could she rise to the challenge? Connie wondered despondently. She didn't know how to help herself, let alone others. She felt a complete failure—and if her Creator was watching, that somehow made it worse: just one more person she had let down.

'Let's go,' she said, getting up stiffly. 'I can sense the others approaching.'

They returned to the entrance of the mines. Darkness had already fallen, pierced by a scattering of stars.

Connie looked up and felt her spirits lift. Stardust. It was an amazing thought: her bones contained the same stuff that made the Milky Way. Was that just chance or was there a plan behind it all, as Gard believed?

Two shadows rippled over the stars, blocking their light for a brief moment before Argot and Skylark circled down to land in the valley.

'We've checked the surroundings. Everyone has gone home. We have the place to ourselves,' Dr Brock announced, sliding nimbly down from the crimson dragon.

Skylark snorted and nudged Connie with a wet kiss from his nose.

'I have missed you, Universal,' he told her. Connie stroked his cheek affectionately.

There was an air of expectation as the friends gathered in a circle around Connie at the entrance to the mines. She sat at the feet of the minotaur with his hands resting on her shoulders. Dr Brock leant back against Argot and closed his eyes. Col buried his head in Skylark's mane. Gard stood, feet apart, eyes bent to the rocky ground. Connie began to shiver but Sentinel increased his grip to steady her.

'Do not fear,' he said softly. 'I have never led anyone astray.'

'It's not that. I'm just afraid of what you'll lead them to,' she replied.

But it was too late to turn back now. Connie closed her eyes and began to feel out for the mythical creatures. Sentinel she found swiftly, waiting for her at the gateway to her mind. Argot flew in to her thoughts confidently, landing at the minotaur's side. Gard emerged between them as if he had always been there and had just been waiting for her to notice. Last to arrive was Skylark, who circled down and landed with a clatter. Connie sensed that with the winged creatures came their companions. As she thought this, she found she could see them, shadows of their real selves sitting on the backs of their mythical creatures.

'Welcome,' Connie said to her guests. 'You may go in.'

Connie imagined opening a gate for them to pass through into her mind. The shadow-door swung open and Sentinel stepped forward.

'This way.' He raised his arm and a torch leapt into life in his hand.

Col had never experienced anything so uncanny as this journey into Connie's mental world. Part of him was fully aware that he was sitting on Skylark's back, head forward on his mount's neck, but the rest of him was deep in an intricate labyrinth, more complex than any mine system he had ever heard of, full of strange branches and circular paths that seemed to bring them back to the same point. At one stage, the minotaur appeared to lose his way and stood for many minutes in silent thought.

Gard gazed at the rock of the walls that surrounded them. 'We are not deep enough yet,' he called. 'These are the superficial levels in the universal's mines—ones I've visited frequently. We must go deeper.'

Sentinel lifted his head. 'I have it.' Taking a passage to the right, they came upon a rough stair winding downwards, disappearing far beyond the feeble light of their torches.

'What if she doesn't want to show us what's down there?' the shadow-Col whispered to Dr Brock as they followed the others.

'I don't know,' the dragon companion replied, watching as the mist of a dream curled around his ankles, glittering with strange lights.

'She can throw us out or trap us for ever any time she wishes,' said the minotaur, overhearing their debate. 'It is her labyrinth—she governs it.'

'Oh no,' muttered Col, his heart racing. He just

hoped that whatever had got into his friend recently was sleeping at the moment.

Gard tapped the wall. A musical tone like a bass note on an organ echoed around the tunnel.

'We are approaching the deepest layers,' he said. 'Prepare yourselves!'

Against what? wondered Col.

Leaving the stairwell, the explorers came out into a vast hall—its size suggesting that this was the most important place in Connie's mind. In front of them stretched a huge expanse of smooth rock wall. But the wall was not bare like all the others they had passed: it was a riot of figures painted in reds and blacks. In one corner, a stick man fought with a bull; a winged horse flew across the smudged sky, chasing the whipping tail of a dragon; ripples of water waved along the bottom edge, rising at intervals into human shapes; a many-armed creature burst out of one side, its limbs flailing; snakes writhed in a halo around a woman's head, her eyes like blazing suns. These and other creatures swirled in and out of each other, many lost in the shadows beyond the torchlight—a record of each of the universal's encounters. But Col had eyes for none of these. He, like his companions, was drawn to the centre of the wall. There, in the very heart of the mural was a great blackness, empty of life. Just looking into it from a distance drained all energy from him and yet he felt inexorably drawn to it. He could not tell if it was solid or not. He took a step nearer. Now he could hear a faint whispering and a wash of waves. A cold breeze was blowing out of the emptiness and ruffling his hair. It reminded him of something—something he could not quite remember.

'What is it?' asked Skylark.

The minotaur grunted. 'It is the secret. But what it is, I do not know.'

Gard took a step forward and raised his mallet to tap on it. Light from the minotaur's torch glinted blood red on the edge of the hammer.

'No!' said Col quickly, grabbing Gard's arm. His fellow travellers turned to stare at him in surprise, Gard with the mallet still lifted in his right hand. The whispering emptiness was suddenly very familiar. 'I know what it is! Don't touch it!'

An orange light flickered briefly on the walls behind Col, before dying out in a hiss of steam.

'I've been here before. It's his mark. It's Kullervo's companionship.'

Gard dropped the mallet with a clatter.

'I had it in me before Connie rescued me last year. Can't you hear it?' Col stopped speaking, listening intently to the foul hiss of Kullervo's breath in his ears. 'This is the answer: I'm sure of it. He's never broken off his link with Connie.'

The room quaked and they were cast out of the labyrinth.

To Connie, witnessing her friends' journey was like being a puppeteer looking down on his theatre. She saw them stumble through the tunnels and knew she could change the scenery if she so wished, place new obstacles in their path or surround them in a bewildering fog, but instead she concentrated all

144

her might on resisting the temptation to interfere. This became particularly difficult when they came upon the wall of cave paintings. She was drawn to the dark blot at its centre and wished that Gard would indeed touch it and rouse whatever was hiding there. She felt a flash of annoyance at Col for stopping him. To her alarm, she could see her anger racing down the tunnels like tongues of fire, about to leap out and punish him, but she quickly quelled the feeling, extinguishing the blaze with streams of water that came gushing out of the labyrinth walls at her call.

On hearing Col put Kullervo's name to the mark, Connie felt a jolt of revulsion and abruptly broke her bond with her companions. Their shadow-selves were thrown out of her mind without a second to prepare themselves for ejection.

Col's head was spinning: he felt as if he had just missed a stair in the dark and tumbled all the way to the bottom. He slid from the back of Skylark who swayed unsteadily on his legs. Dr Brock gave a small groan and sat up, his eyes now open. The minotaur had his head in his hands.

'Sorry,' said Connie. 'I didn't mean to do that so quickly.'

They remained silent. Connie wished someone would speak—return the atmosphere to normality so that the horror of what they had just discovered about her would be lessened.

Gard spoke first: 'What we saw explains many things. It explains why an encounter with another creature rouses Connie from what she is doing—it takes her to another part of that wall and away from his mark.'

'Yes, Kullervo appears to be entering when her defences are down—like when she is asleep,' said Dr Brock.

Or when I'm feeling strong negative emotion, such as anger, added Connie to herself, remembering the storm she had summoned on the night of the wedding.

'But how can he be doing this when we know he's on the other side of the earth?' asked Col. 'He's in Japan or somewhere, isn't he?'

Gard tapped his mallet on the ground. 'In some encounters, physical proximity is not necessary. I can reach Connie wherever she is as long as her feet touch the earth. Kullervo has claimed her as his own companion—their bond is strong.'

'And we don't know that he *is* in the Far East for certain,' said Dr Brock. 'We only know that his supporters are.'

'So he could've sent them there as a diversion from what he is doing here?' asked Col eagerly.

'Possibly,' said Dr Brock, 'but he has many plans and we do not understand them all.'

Gard stamped over to the minotaur and grasped his hand. 'Thank you, my friend, you have done us a great service. We must take our findings to the Trustees and I have no doubt that they will want to see what we have discovered for themselves. Will you be ready to offer your skills again to us?'

'If the universal wishes it,' Sentinel replied. 'I am her sentinel, not theirs.'

'I'll let you know,' said Connie. At the moment, all she wanted to do was run away and sleep. It was tiring enough sustaining multiple bonds without having to bear the shame of your innermost secrets being revealed to other eyes. If she could, she would have stepped outside herself, leaving everything behind, including that foul mark, like a snake shedding a skin. But she couldn't escape it—it was too deep. Kullervo would always be with her. The thought tormented her.

'And you, Companion to Pegasi, you must be our authority on this,' said Gard, turning to Col, 'as your experience comes closest to what is happening to the universal.'

'If that's so,' said Col, 'then I can tell you that Kullervo uses what you have inside you, what you normally keep bottled up. In my case it turned out to be cruelty and violence.'

'So in my case, it's the desire to create chaos and harm others?' asked Connie, appalled.

'I don't think so,' said Dr Brock gently. 'I don't think your intention was to harm us with that thunderbolt. I think we appeared to you in that state no more than ants in the way of your boot, or flies to swat.'

'So what was I doing then?' asked Connie, not sure that this explanation was in any way reassuring.

'Connie, you have great powers but you normally resist the temptation to abuse them. You were allowing these powers out to play. Perhaps we should only be surprised that you don't exercise them more often.'

'But what can we do for Connie?' asked Col. 'We can't leave her with the fear that Kullervo might break through again.'

'No,' said Gard, 'but I think we must go on as we have begun: make sure Connie is surrounded by friends. You have Argand with you in your bedroom when you sleep, do you not?'

'Yes,' said Connie. The little dragon curled up at the end of her bed each night, providing Connie with both the comfort of her presence and the warmth for her cold feet.

'That is good: her bond must now be quite strong as she is your special companion—hopefully your connection with her is strong enough to counter that of Kullervo.'

Connie nodded, though she felt instinctively that no bond could defeat the one she had with the shape-shifter, even Argand with whom she spent the most time. Kullervo, as she had reluctantly learned last year, was her counterpart in the mythical world—in some strange way, they needed each other.

'We must make sure that you never sleep alone and place creatures to guard you at your most vulnerable times,' Gard continued. 'If you slept outdoors, I could be with you, of course, but I doubt you'd want to exchange your mattress to lie under the winter sky.'

'Er . . . no, but thanks for the offer,' said Connie. 'Argand will be fine for now—until she gets too big to get in and out of the window.'

An owl hooted in the trees of the plantation.

'It's getting very late,' said Dr Brock, 'we must take our young people home.'

'There's just one thing I don't understand,' said Col.

'Just one?' Connie asked wryly.

'Maybe not,' Col conceded. 'But what I wanted to ask you, Connie, is why, if you freed me from Kullervo's bond last year, you can't do the same for yourself?'

'How do you know you don't have the same mark deep inside you, young man?' growled the minotaur. 'Have you ever stopped to look?'

Col shuddered. He hadn't thought of that.

'I don't think he has,' said Connie wearily. 'Kullervo's occupation of Col was not a true bond. I saw no sign of it when I visited his mind: I only sensed Kullervo's presence as a kind of atmosphere— like a storm battering the normal stuff in Col's head. I think I was able to blow it away when I used the helm—that's one of the universal's tools—on Col. It protected his mind from Kullervo's attack.'

'So, Connie, can't you put the helm on again— for yourself this time?' Col asked.

'I don't know. It might work—but only when I'm awake and know what I'm doing.'

'Even the most hardy warrior must lay aside his armour to sleep,' growled Argot.

'Yes,' said Dr Brock, understanding his companion's thought, 'you must not be afraid to sleep, Connie. No one can survive like that.'

'But what really worries me,' admitted Connie, 'is that the mark you saw is within my defences. I doubt now that either my shield or helm could reach it. I'd be shutting it in, not blocking it out.'

'That remains to be seen. All we can do now is ensure that by our vigilance you are not again in a position where you need to find that out,' said Gard.

11

Letters

Rat was eager to hear from Connie and Col what had happened with the minotaur. He was duly impressed by the description of the journey in the mind's labyrinth when Col told him the details at school on Monday. It was lunchtime and Connie was sitting silently on the other side, not eating very much, allowing Col to do the talking.

'Amazing!' said Rat, turning to stare at Connie. 'You mean she's got this great black hole in her? You wouldn't think it to look at her.'

'Thanks, Rat,' said Connie ironically. 'I'm flattered.'

'But all that power! I can't get over it.'

'Get over it,' said Col in a terse voice. 'Connie doesn't need you treating her like a freak show.'

As usual, the rebuff washed over Rat. 'Can I come next time?'

'Come?' asked Connie, perplexed.

'Visit your cave paintings, or whatever they are.'

'No you can't,' she said firmly. 'I'm not having Icefen loping around inside my head.'

'You're probably right. I couldn't guarantee he wouldn't give you permanent amnesia or something if he breathed in the wrong place.'

Col gave Rat a nudge to make him shut up as Jane and Anneena approached with their trays.

'Hi, guys,' said Anneena, wiggling in between Col and Connie.

Jane perched on the end of the bench. 'Have you heard? They've started building the wind farm.'

'Oh yeah, we saw,' said Col grumpily.

'You saw and didn't tell me!' exclaimed Anneena, scandalized by his failure to keep her up-to-date with the local gossip.

'Sorry, we had other things on our minds,' said Connie.

Rat laughed but Col still looked grim-faced. He toyed with his meal, remembering the pegasi's failed protest; some of the winged creatures were even threatening to leave the Society over the scheme. Dr Brock and the others had said they had to go with the majority view—and most creatures had been in favour thanks to Rat and Icefen's vigorous campaign among the members, culminating in the universal's decision to back it. Connie's vote had swayed many creatures who had been unable to make up their minds.

'Why so angry, Col?' asked Jane, offering around her crisps. 'Isn't it good that the wind farm is being built?'

'Good for who?' he countered. 'For us humans? Yeah, I s'pose. But why do we always have to come first?'

Jane looked puzzled. 'I don't understand: who else cares about it other than humans?'

Col realized he had given too much away. 'I dunno. It's just that we seem to be taking more and more for ourselves—now we've even started stealing the skies.'

'We started that long ago,' said Rat.

'Still, I think it's not going to be too bad once it's finished,' commented Anneena, waving her fork in a circle in the air. 'Might even look beautiful in its own way. I wouldn't mind going to see it.'

'Yeah, why don't you come round after school?' suggested Rat. 'But don't say anything to my ma about liking wind farms. She thinks the masts are the spawn of the devil and spends most of her day shouting at the builders. Mr Masterson seems to be steering clear of our cottage or else she'd have a go at him too, I expect.'

Anneena laughed. 'I consider myself forewarned. Do you want to come, Connie?'

'I'd better not.' Connie had no wish to run into Mr Masterson again.

'Why not?' Anneena asked in surprise. 'I thought you'd like to call on your uncle.'

'Connie and I are busy,' said Col, covering for her. 'Promised to do something for Gran.'

'I'd like to come,' said Jane. 'I'll bring my camera.'

'Great. If you come, I can show you both around a bit.' Rat's eyes were glinting with his most wolfish expression. He looked as if he was plotting something.

'You won't introduce them to any of your *friends*, will you, Rat?' asked Connie anxiously. 'You know Anneena doesn't feel comfortable with Wolf, don't you?'

'Not like Wolf!' he exclaimed. 'Then I'll have to show her that he's just a harmless puppy compared to—'

Col jumped up. 'Time to go. Must get to Maths early to get a good seat.' He dragged Rat away, lunch only half-eaten.

Jane shook her head. 'Is Col feeling all right? I've never known him rush to Mrs Stephens's class.'

'Well, there's always a first time for everything,' said Anneena.

When Connie arrived home that afternoon, she found that the cliff at the back of the beach beyond Shaker Row had been wreathed in red and white striped tape. It fluttered in the breeze as if marking out a crime scene. Two men with yellow helmets could be seen on the top probing the earth with an instrument that looked like a metal detector. Dumping her bag in the kitchen, Connie discovered Evelyn sitting alone at the table, her head bent over her laptop computer. A brown envelope addressed to Mack sat unopened in the toast rack.

'Where's Mack?' asked Connie, putting on the kettle.

'The Kraken's down near Plymouth. He's gone for a swim.'

'Ah,' said Connie with sudden comprehension. Thinking about it, she could feel a faint echo of the presence of the Kraken in her mind. 'So, what's going on outside then?'

'The council have decided the cliffs are unsafe,' Evelyn said, her lips compressed in a thin line.

'Are they unsafe?' asked Connie reasonably, helping herself to a biscuit from the battered tin on the dresser.

'I don't know. I've not noticed any changes to them. Have you?'

'No, but I'm not sure I'd know if anything was wrong.'

Evelyn pushed the computer away. 'I'm writing to the council now to say so—not that it'll do much good. They're going to look at the cliffs behind our cottages next. We'll probably come home to find our house roped off tomorrow.'

'Whatever for?'

The kettle clicked off and Evelyn got up to make the tea. 'The man said that they'd become worried because the storms in November and December had been more severe than usual and caused damage all along the coast. Previously sound cliffs had had to be declared unsafe. They didn't want anyone to be killed should it happen again.'

'But that was me! It won't happen again, I promise!'

Evelyn smiled. 'I could hardly say to the man from the council, "Oh, excuse me but my niece is a storm-raiser and has given me her word not to use her great powers again", now could I?'

'I s'pose not. So what are we going to do?'

'Do? I don't know if there's anything we can do. Wait for the council's verdict, I suppose.'

Connie leant against the dresser despondently. Her eyes travelled over their collection of bric-a-brac and lighted on a piece of jet once given her by Gard.

'There is something we can do,' she said. 'It's obvious—we've a rock dwarf as a houseguest, we'll put him on to it.'

Col's house was empty when he returned from school. His grandmother was at her Women's Institute meeting, pretending to be a normal senior citizen like most of her non-Society friends. At least it meant that she had done some baking and left her grandson a supply of scones for his tea. Col wolfed one down, not bothering with the china plate she had optimistically put out for him. He noticed that she had also left out a brown envelope propped up against the jam. It had the initials SPMC stamped across the top and his name on the front. He tore the letter open:

'Dear Mr Clamworthy, Companion to Pegasi

It has been brought to our attention that you have broken the ban on further communication with the former Society member, Connie Lionheart. You were seen in her company on 11 January in the presence of a rock dwarf. I wish to remind you that the conditions of her expulsion clearly state that she is no longer to have any contact with mythical creatures and your presence on this occasion indicates that you condoned her violation of this decision. Similar letters have been sent to all others present at the scene.

I am writing therefore to issue an official warning. I have also informed your mentor of your serious misconduct and I have requested that he take the necessary disciplinary steps. Any further such incident will result in your suspension for an indefinite period from the Society.

Yours sincerely,
Ivor Coddrington
Trustee

Go take a running jump, Ivor Coddrington, was Col's first thought. He threw the letter angrily onto the table. Slumping into a chair, he found he had lost his appetite for the scones. Picking the letter up again, he read it through more carefully. This time the phrase that most struck him was the one that said that his mentor had been asked to take disciplinary measures. Col knew that Captain Graves was a stickler for the rules: he would not look kindly on the activities of the pro-Connie faction. What kind of punishment would he think necessary? Whatever it was, Col knew he was not going to like it.

Mack's reaction to his letter of reprimand was to threaten to hang it up in the downstairs loo and invite anyone to use it when they ran out of paper. Connie was relieved to find that he did not blame her in the least for his official warning.

157

'It's not the first I've received,' he said with a hint of pride.

'Nor the last,' added Evelyn behind his back.

Connie spent the night wondering why Gard had not received a letter from Mr Coddrington despite the fact he was openly staying at their house. She half expected it to drop through the letterbox the next morning and so looked up apprehensively as her aunt came into the kitchen with the post.

'Nothing for Gard then?' Connie asked as her aunt split the pile in two; the larger half she kept for herself, a single letter she chucked at Mack who caught it deftly in his left hand.

Gard grunted with derision from the armchair by the fireplace where Madame Cresson had curled up on his knee. He did not eat or drink but he liked to keep them company at breakfast. 'Coddrington knows better than to take me on, Universal,' he said, understanding her thought. 'I still command respect for my frequent periods of service as Trustee over the centuries: he knows that.'

'Whereas insignificant rebels like me and my son, he doesn't care two hoots about, is that it, Rock Dwarf?' Mack said with a laugh.

'That is it, Kraken Companion,' returned Gard in the same spirit. 'Though I am surprised a Sea Snake, reputed by his nearest and dearest to have frogspawn for brains, was so quick to see to the heart of the matter.'

'Frogspawn!' exclaimed Mack, turning on Evelyn. 'You didn't say that, did you?'

'No,' said Evelyn innocently, 'don't look at me

like that. I wish I had said it though . . .'

'It was your mother,' Gard butted in.

'The treachery of women!' Mack said, casting his hands up in the air dramatically. He threw himself at Connie's feet. 'Connie, it's up to you to save the reputation of your sex and denounce all these foul slurs on my intelligence.'

'Oh, I don't know, Mack,' Connie said hesitantly, still unused to the ways of her new uncle, 'frogspawn sounds a lot safer than what I've got in my head. I'd stick with that if I were you.'

He laughed. 'True, I forgot I was having breakfast with our own weapon of mass destruction.'

Connie gave a wan smile. 'Yeah, you're a brave man to risk it.'

Gard was clearly uncomfortable with the turn the conversation had taken. His joints creaked in the chair as he turned round to address Evelyn who was immersed in her letters at the far end of the table.

'What were you saying last night, Evelyn, about your cliff?'

Evelyn looked up. 'It was Connie's idea. She thought you might be able to help.'

'Oh, yeah,' said Connie putting down her spoon, 'I just thought you might be able to check out the cliff for us—you know, tell us if it's dangerous or not. Is there anything you can do about it?'

Gard nodded slowly. 'Perhaps. I will investigate for you.'

There was a knock at the back door. Mack moved quickly to stand in front of Gard as Evelyn opened the door a crack.

'Mrs Evelyn Lionheart?' enquired a man's voice on the other side.

'Yes?' Evelyn replied, her shoulders blocking his view into the kitchen.

'I tried the front but there was no answer.'

'That's right: the bell's not worked for decades. How can I help you?'

'I'm from the council. We'd like to discuss relocation with you.'

'Relocation? I'm not going anywhere.'

'We're not talking about anything permanent. Just a temporary measure while we look at the cliff and see if we can make it safe—'

'Examine away,' she said, starting to close the door, 'but I'll take care of myself, thanks.'

The man appeared to have wedged his foot in the door. 'I was warned you wouldn't like it—nobody would, of course—but I don't think you quite understand. We are about to declare the cliff unsafe and that means you'll have to move out, like it or not. You've got a child here, I believe. Social Services will not look kindly on you putting her life at risk, whatever you do with your own.'

Evelyn threw the door open again, this time wide so that the bespectacled man from the council obtained a clear view of the kitchen. In a flash, Mack pulled Connie over to his side to create a larger barrier for the rock dwarf.

'Don't you threaten me with Social Services!' Evelyn said in a menacing tone.

'My dear lady, I'm not threatening you! But you must know that your situation has been discussed by the council. Your niece is well known to Social Services—my word, even I know about her after her running away last year and I'm nothing to do with that department!'

'Well, if it's nothing to do with you, Mr . . . ?'

'Cornell.'

'Mr Cornell, then I suggest you say nothing about it.'

'Face facts, Mrs Lionheart,' Mr Cornell said in a final effort to get through to her, 'you'll have to move.'

'No, you face facts. That cliff is not yet declared unsafe and may never be. My family is staying put.' She slammed the door.

'Well,' said Gard, getting to his feet with a creak, 'I had better start work. It looks as if you need some mythical help to sort this one out.'

Col approached the Mastersons' farm on Tuesday evening with a feeling of trepidation. His breath came in white clouds as he pedalled along the dark country lane, his bike lights dancing off the verges. Captain Graves had left an urgent message demanding Col's presence at a meeting to discuss his conduct so he knew he was in for trouble. It was with feelings akin to a prisoner going to his sentencing that he stacked his bike against the barn wall and went in search of his mentor.

Knocking on the back door of the farmhouse, Col found himself face to face with Shirley, Mr Masterson's daughter. She gave him a smug smile as she held the door open for him.

'Hi, Col,' she said, 'Captain Graves is expecting you. He's in the dining room with Dad.' She flicked her long blonde hair over her shoulder—having met her Cousin Erik, Col now understood from which side of the family she got her pale colouring.

'Oh,' said Col shortly, pulling off his gloves and jacket, adding them to the miscellaneous collection of coats in the corner of the kitchen. His jacket promptly slid off its peg but he could not be bothered to pick it up.

'She's not worth it, you know,' Shirley said, returning to the magazine she had been reading at the kitchen table.

'What?' Col rapped back, stung into anger by her tone.

'Connie Lionheart. "Hescombe's only universal." The Society doesn't need universals any more. They just put the rest of us at risk. If I were you, I wouldn't sacrifice my training to keep in with her.'

Trying to master his annoyance, Col took a deep breath, knowing that an outburst at Shirley just prior to facing a disciplinary hearing was not the wisest course of action.

'Well, Shirley,' he said, his voice only trembling slightly as he put on a passing imitation of a conversational tone, 'at least I now know one thing.'

'Oh yes?' enquired Shirley, putting her magazine aside in expectation of hearing his change of heart. She smiled flirtatiously at him. 'Seen the error of your ways, Col? I always knew you were smart.'

'Oh, I'm smart all right,' said Col with a hard

smile, 'but now I know that you're not. You must be thick to think the Society can get by ignoring the fact that there's a universal out there. Anyway, Connie's my friend and I stick by my friends, unlike some people I know.'

He kicked open the door out of the kitchen and left before she had a chance to say any more—not because he was afraid of an argument but because he was afraid he would enjoy it too much and live to regret giving vent to his feelings.

He knocked firmly on the dining room door, in no mood to show contrition.

'Come in, Col,' said Captain Graves sternly.

His mentor and Mr Masterson were sitting next to each other on the far side of the polished table.

'Sit down,' said Captain Graves, waving at a chair opposite him. 'You know why you're here, of course?'

Col nodded, choosing to sit down rather than answer. He had already decided that the least he said the better. Mr Masterson was looking at him with an expression of regret mixed with self-righteousness.

'Mr Masterson has done his duty by bringing your misconduct to the attention of the Trustees,' said Captain Graves, with a nod at his neighbour, 'though he has also stressed to me that you were less to blame than the adults you were with. You cannot be expected to go against the wishes of your father or of others you are used to trusting.'

Col looked down at his fingers, noting absently how dirty his nails were. He could tell that Mr Masterson and Captain Graves, both kindly men in the right circumstances, were attempting to give him a way out.

'It may be that you were merely following their wishes when you went on your expedition with Connie Lionheart and the rock dwarf last Saturday?' suggested Captain Graves, his eyes glinting at Col from under his grey brows.

Col said nothing but began to pick the grime from his thumbnail.

Captain Graves rubbed his moustache speculatively. 'On the other hand, perhaps you fully condoned their action and have no intention of obeying the Society's ban against your friend?'

Col still said nothing but stopped digging at his nails.

'In which case, you are in serious trouble. Rules are there to keep our mythical creatures safe. They must be obeyed, however painful that may prove to us individually. We all have to learn that the good of the whole is more important than our private feelings on a matter.'

Col felt the urge to argue with his mentor. It was so tempting to speak his mind. But he mustn't. He gripped his hands tightly, trying to keep the lid on his anger.

'Connie's a nice enough girl, I've no doubt, and probably very persuasive with a warm-hearted boy like yourself,' Captain Graves continued, his eyes fixed on the top of his charge's bent head. 'I've no doubt she's talked you into thinking she should be given another chance. You've probably even forgiven her for trying to kill you.'

'She's done no such thing,' Col said, each word an effort as he struggled to keep cool. 'She's not asked me for anything.'

'What! Not even your forgiveness!' said Mr Masterson with a hollow laugh. 'It's a strange kind of girl who can try to blast her best friends apart and not worry about it afterwards.'

'Of course, she's worried about it!' Col spat out, but then pulled back, regaining control. 'But what she's said about it to me is private.'

'Oh ho!' said Captain Graves knowingly. 'I thought as much. When I heard that my star pupil was abusing the Society in this way, I thought that it had to be a matter of the heart rather than the head. You see, Clive,' he said, turning to Mr Masterson, 'it's as I said: the poor boy can't think straight about her.'

'What?' Col sat up, staring at his mentor.

'Don't worry, my boy, I remember what first love was like,' said Captain Graves with a paternal smile. 'And I dare say Clive does too.'

'Oh yes,' said Mr Masterson with a sigh.

Col looked from one to the other in amazement. Both of them were now wearing inane grins and looking at him as if he were to be pitied. The penny dropped.

'Connie's my friend,' he said. 'We're just good friends.'

'That's what they all say, isn't it, Michael?' said Mr Masterson with a wink.

'But it's true!' Col thundered back.

Mr Masterson and Captain Graves refused to be angry with him and continued to smile at each other.

'Unfortunately, Col, you'll have to learn to curb your feelings for the former Society member if you are to remain on the training programme,' said Captain Graves gently. 'But as it was a first offence, I'll be merciful and only ground you for a month.'

'A month!' Col protested.

'It will delay your Grade Four examination a year unfortunately, but that's the penalty you have to pay. However, if I hear you have been associating with Miss Lionheart again,' Captain Graves continued, his voice taking on a hard edge, 'I'm afraid I'll have to suspend your training and inform the Trustees that you should not be allowed near the pegasi until you have proved that you can obey Society rules.'

There was a moment in which Col knew he had a choice: either he could accept the sentence and leave the room or he could give vent to his anger and tell them exactly what he thought of them both. Looking up at the family portraits on the walls, all of which seemed to be listening with the same supercilious smile of their descendant, Shirley, Col knew that he would not give them the pleasure of seeing him lose control. That was what Connie had done in this very same room, admittedly under worse provocation, and she had ended up with an expulsion. He swallowed and said nothing.

'Do you understand, Col?' asked Captain Graves severely.

Col nodded, still gazing hard at one bald-headed Masterson from the past, concentrating on his ugly bulbous nose.

'Then I hope to see you again in mid-February. I'll explain to Skylark why you are unable to train with him. I'll find someone else to ride in your place for a few weeks so that he can continue with his training programme.'

This was the hardest moment of all: hearing that his place on Skylark's back was to be taken by some other pegasus rider. Col dug his nails into the palm of his hand to prevent himself saying anything, focusing instead on the pain he was inflicting on himself.

'Then I look forward to seeing you in a few weeks. Oh, and . . . er . . . let her down gently, won't you, my boy?' Captain Graves said, standing up and picking his cane up off the table. 'She must be having a hard time and I've always rather liked her myself. But duty is duty.' He pointed to the door.

Col shuffled to his feet. 'I can go then?'

'Dismissed,' said Captain Graves briskly as he always did at the end of a training session, but this time adding, 'and good luck. If you need any tips on what to say, I imagine Clive here would be happy to make some suggestions. He was quite a ladies' man himself in his day, as I remember.'

'Get on with you, Michael,' said Mr Masterson, blushing.

'Thanks, but I'll be fine,' Col said, leaving quickly before Mr Masterson felt moved to share any reminiscences of his past love affairs with him. It was only when he was outside in the cold night air that he realized he had apparently confirmed their suspicions about him and Connie with his last remark. It was too late now to go back in. The absurdity of the situation made him give a mirthless laugh as he pedalled back home, already resolved that no one should hear anything about it. He would not be able to live it down if Rat got hold of it.

12

Snowstorm

Col and Rat were walking down the top corridor a few steps behind Connie on their way to Geography.

'So, Col, what's all this about you and Connie?' asked Rat.

Col grabbed his friend by the front of his jumper and bundled him into the caretaker's store cupboard. Connie, who had turned round on hearing her name mentioned, was just in time to see Rat being jerked inside and the door banged shut.

'What did you say?' hissed Col fiercely, still gripping Rat's grey pullover. Rat wriggled free.

'Hey, cool it!' Rat brushed himself down and perched on an empty shelf. 'Touchy!'

'I'm not touchy,' Col growled back, 'but you'd better tell me why you said that—and now!'

'All right, all right, keep your hair on.' Rat was trying hard not to laugh at his friend's expression of outrage. 'I just heard from Erik that you've been told to dump Connie. Strange,' he added reflectively, 'I hadn't even realized you two were going out and now it's all over.'

'It's not all over,' replied Col, kicking a bucket angrily, making the cupboard ring with its dull chime.

'So you've not dumped her yet?' said Rat eagerly, his bright eyes twinkling in the semi-darkness.

'Aargh!' Col let out an exasperated groan. 'Course it's not all over—it never started. It's just a figment of my mentor's overactive imagination.'

'Oh, I see,' said Rat sceptically.

'And if you tell Connie one word about all this, I'll kill you!'

'As if I would!' Rat grinned back.

There was a tap at the door before someone pulled it open.

'Col, Rat, are you OK?' It was Connie peering anxiously in on them.

'We're fine, Connie,' said Rat brightly. 'It's just Col suffering from the effects of an overactive imagination.'

'I'm not,' Col grunted.

'What?' Connie looked puzzled.

'Forget it,' said Col, quickly leaving the cupboard, pulling Rat with him. 'Come on, we're going to be late.'

The threesome began to jog down the now deserted corridor. Checking no one was within earshot, Connie asked Rat: 'So how was your visit to the wind farm with Jane and Anneena? They didn't come across anything unexpected, did they?'

'Oh no,' said Rat. 'I kept Icefen away from them. Course, he caught their scent from the plantation and was itching to give them a fright, but I made him promise to behave. Besides, with all those builders up there, it'd be loads of people to knock out. We might've missed someone.'

'Yeah,' said Connie, relieved but not entirely comforted by hearing of her friends' near escape.

'You should come up there again, Connie,' Rat continued. 'The masts are going up. They're really cool.' He glanced at Col. 'Even Ma thinks they're not so bad now she's seen them. At least, she's stopped swearing at the foreman, which is a relief for Dad. Mr Masterson asked him to control Ma—doesn't understand a thing about women, that man.'

'Perhaps I will,' said Connie as they turned into the Geography corridor. 'I'll go and see Uncle Hugh on Saturday and take a look. Even Mr Masterson can't object to me visiting him. Will you be flying, Col?'

'Er . . . no,' said Col shortly.

Connie paused at the classroom door and turned to him in surprise.

'Whyever not? You always fly at the weekend, don't you?'

'He's been grounded,' Rat chipped in. 'Are you going to open this door, Connie, or do I have to climb over you?'

Connie ignored him. 'Grounded?'

'Yeah, my punishment,' said Col.

'For what?'

'For going out . . . sorry, for hanging out with you,' Rat said.

Connie dropped her hand from the door.

'Oh, Col, I'm so sorry.'

'Forget it,' Col muttered.

'You'll land us in more trouble if you don't move,' Rat said, pushing her aside to open the door. As the three of them entered, Connie distinctly heard Rat mutter to Col, 'I never understood what you saw in her, in any case.' Col gave him a shove in the back so that Rat half-stumbled into the class.

Gard had a grim report to make at supper that evening.

'I have examined the cliff,' he told Evelyn. 'And I'm afraid that the council's worries are not entirely unfounded. There has been serious erosion of the coast over the years but Hescombe itself is usually sheltered from the worst by the headland. But the particular stretch near your house tells a strange story. It has been quiet for some twenty years or so, according to the rock. There is a memory of frequent poundings before that time, but then nothing until a few months ago. Very strange.'

'It's not strange,' said Evelyn, stirring her lentil soup slowly. 'I remember the storms when I was young. My aunt always used to love rough weather because it brought her white horses out of their stables. She'd stand on the beach and call to them. I used to watch from the attic bedroom as they threw themselves at her. Many of them used to overshoot and dash themselves against the cliff in their game. It was amazing to watch.'

'And she died twenty years ago, I suppose?' said Gard.

'Yes—twenty years ago this January when I was only sixteen. I wish I'd had her with me for many more years—it was incredibly difficult for us both. She discharged herself from hospital at the end— told the doctors she wanted to die with the sound of waves in her ears.' Evelyn smiled sadly.

'I released the white horses from their stables in November,' Connie admitted in a subdued voice. 'So it's my fault, isn't it?'

Gard sighed. 'Erosion happens all the time, Connie. It is the way of the sea and the rock to mingle and part in an eternal shifting of the sands. Though, I must admit,' he said with a shake of his head, 'mankind has made it happen much faster of late.'

'But not here. You said it was sheltered here.'

'I did. And yes, you have unwittingly caused some damage,' he acknowledged reluctantly.

'But can it be repaired?'

'It will be difficult. I will have to talk to the stone sprites.' Connie gave an involuntary shudder, remembering the cold touch of some of her least favourite mythical creatures, encountered in Mallins Wood.

'What, those things!' Mack spluttered in his soup. He too remembered the stone sprites. It was hard to forget creatures that had tried to freeze you to death. 'Well, we'd better pack our bags then.'

'No,' said Gard firmly. 'You do not understand them as I do. They do not usually like to help, but they have the power to firm the rock and fill the cracks. If they see that it will be to their advantage, they might assist us.'

'Advantage?' queried Evelyn. 'What possible advantage could they see in keeping my house safe?'

'They would earn the gratitude of the universal. Even they, cold and heartless as they are, hunger for the universal. With Connie's help, I will be able to talk to them. As long as the cliffs are free from any attack until we have had time to shore it up, then I think we need not pack our bags.'

'OK,' said Connie. 'When shall we do it?'

'The sooner the better. I suggest tomorrow morning,' said Gard.

Connie nodded. 'Can't say I'm looking forward to it.'

Gard gave a hoarse laugh. 'Come, come, Universal, there is more to the life of a stone than you yet know. You need your horizons broadened.'

'So it seems,' she muttered glumly.

The wind whistled around the eaves disturbing Connie from her sleep. Argand shifted uneasily, snout twitching as she felt the sudden drop in air pressure. Awake now, Connie lay looking at the ceiling, comforted by the glow of warmth from her slumbering companion. She listened to the rain pattering on the slates. The drumming sound faded but the wind still moaned. Connie sat up, wondering if the rain had passed. Her temples were aching. Taking a sip of water, she got out of bed, thinking to go down and find an aspirin. She pulled on a dressing gown and wandered over to the window, shivering in the cold as she drew back the curtain. The rain had stopped but only because it was now falling as soundless snow. The wind was blowing the flakes in flurries this way and that like a demented sheepdog worrying his flock. A full moon shone out then disappeared quickly behind cloud. Its glow revealed a sea whipped to a frenzy, white crests racing for the shore and crashing onto the beach.

Connie stood frozen to the spot, her mission to fetch an aspirin forgotten. The crests were curling over and taking the shape of horses galloping towards the shore. Who had called them? It could not have been her this time as she was wide awake! What was more, if the white horses reached the cliff, who knew what damage they might cause? They might even bring the whole thing crashing down on the house.

Connie clattered down the stairs.

'They're here!' she shouted at the top of her voice to rouse her aunt and Mack. 'Get out of the house!'

Flinging open the front door, Connie slid down the path in her slippers. She jumped onto the shingle and dashed to the water's edge. As waves collided with stones, foam flew into the air, mixing with the swarming snow. Connie's skin was soon red-raw with cold. She was just in time to see a white stallion charge up the beach on course to throw itself at the crumbling foundations of the cliff. Digging deep into her mind for the memory of her last encounter, she sought out the wild rushing presence of the white horse. Her lips formed themselves instinctively into a whistle, summoning it from its suicidal path. Hearing the trilling note, the horse turned from its course and galloped along the beach, heading now for the companion that had called it. Spray flicked into the air from its long mane, dark eyes wide with exhilaration and storm-madness. Bracing herself for the impact, Connie covered her head with her arms. A wall of water crashed on top of her, knocking her to the ground. The horse dissolved back into the element from which it came, departing with the next ebb of the waves. In the moment of contact, Connie caught a glimpse of the true nature of the white horse—a brief tempestuous career through life culminating in frenzied destruction, repeated endlessly in a cycle of death and rebirth.

Staggering to her feet, Connie now saw that a herd of white horses was charging in from the sea, scores of them all heading in her direction. How could she stop them throwing themselves at her? She would be swept away in the impact; some were bound to overshoot and crash into the cliffs. Desperate at least to save her aunt and Mack, she broke into a run, dashing along the beach away from the house. Like an athlete taking first place in a sprint, she burst through the red and white tape that was meant to keep people away from the cliff. It streamed behind her, fluttering in the gale. The lead horses were now only metres from where the waves were breaking on the shore, their whinnies screaming above the howl of the wind. She could not hope to outpace them.

There was a flash of lightning overhead and Connie saw one of the horses illuminated in silver splendour, its nostrils flaring as it scented the end of the race. A dark shadow passed swiftly behind it, edged with white light, and then the horse crashed down upon Connie, burying her in foam and spray. Then another—and another hit her. She was struck from all sides: no sooner had she regained her feet than the next horse threw itself ecstatically upon her, perishing in the delight of encountering a universal. Inexorably, she was sucked further down the beach towards the sea along with the scrabbling pebbles. Trying to crawl back up the strand, she saw through stinging eyes many of the horses colliding with the cliff in front of her, then joining the backwash that undermined her attempt to reach safety. Coughing and retching, she lost her grip and slid into the waves. Just then a rumble gave a split-second's warning of the landslip. A section of the cliff above the beach crumbled onto the pebbles, throwing up lighter grit and sand that spattered around her in the foaming water.

She had no time to consider her narrow escape. The waves had saved her from being buried in the landslide, but she was now in danger of being drowned in the mad enthusiasm of the white horses. Their hooves splashed around her head as each took a turn to collapse onto the companion, drenching her in freezing water. She was kicked and buffeted, stunned by blow after blow, like a fallen jockey tossed under hooves in a steeplechase.

'Stop it!' Connie cried, gasping for air, her nails tearing at the pebbles as they tumbled back with her into the breaking waves. 'Help!'

A hand grasped the neck of her dressing gown and hauled her up. Another hand then pulled her arm. Two men dragged her up the beach.

'Call them off, Connie!' she heard Mack gasp as another white horse collided with them, pushing them back into the suck of the ebb.

'Can't!' she choked. 'I don't know how.'

'Brace!' shouted the other man.

A white mare charged them, hitting Connie squarely in the back and throwing her forward out of their grasp. Mack quickly grabbed her belt to stop her rolling down the shelving pebbles.

'You'd better learn fast!' he shouted at her, his face dripping with spray. 'Because we won't get back otherwise.'

Another horse crashed down upon her, kicking Mack's hand from her waist. Connie tumbled into the water. She gasped for breath, reaching out with her flailing hands and mind to the horses of the storm. She was swept along by their powerful, fatal desire to throw themselves at her and end their short life in a shout of joy: it would take a strong will to curb this urge.

She would need a tool to tame them.

A bridle.

Hovering like a will-o'-the wisp, the silver outline of a harness appeared in her mind.

Connie crawled to her knees in the ebb and cast the bridle over the next horse to race towards her.

The bridle-bond fell in place, bit between teeth. Reluctantly, the mare slowed, bucking and rearing under the unaccustomed restraint. Connie, knee-deep in the undertow, struggled to retain her balance as she whispered calming words to the creature, pulling on the bond between them. Its canter slowed to a trot. As Connie held out her palm, the horse gingerly approached and inclined its head to her hand. The moment its nose touched her skin, it dissolved, disappearing back into the sea, leaving Connie with an imprint of its quiet thrill of pleasure at having encountered another. Now the rest of the herd followed the path of the mare, rolling calmly towards her, touching her, then fading back into the ocean.

Connie had begun to think that she had succeeded in subduing them, but not all the wild white horses of the sea were to be tamed so easily. One horse stood aloof, a magnificent stallion and king of the herd. She reached out to him but he bucked. Front hooves raking the air, he threw off the bit and bridal to leap on top of her, knocking her back into the water. Only the swift reactions of her rescuers saved her. They plucked her out of the backwash before she was swept away and this time they were able to haul her up the beach to safety.

Someone threw a blanket over her shoulders. Shivering violently, Connie looked up and saw that her second saviour was a dark-haired man in a fringed jacket, now soaked to the skin: the Trustee, Eagle-Child. He was glaring down at her, his normally mild eyes bitter with disappointment. By his side, a huge black-feathered bird flickered with angry white light: Storm-Bird. Hooves clopped on the road behind her and Connie spun round to see Kira Okona dismounting from the back of the unicorn, Windfoal. Already landed and waiting under the street lamp outside Number Five crouched the old green dragon, Morjik, and his companion, Kinga Potowska. Then, out of the shadows, stepped the final Trustee, Ivor Coddrington.

'You've seen with your own eyes,' he said triumphantly, 'seen that everything I told you was true. This is why I expelled her; this is why she is a danger to herself and to us all! She must be stopped.'

13

Appeal

'It w-wasn't me,' Connie stuttered through chattering teeth. 'I d-didn't summon this storm.' She remembered her aching temples. 'There was a weather giant out there.'

Mr Coddrington folded his arms and looked down at her, his scorn all too evident. 'Rubbish. There's no weather giant in the vicinity—except Hoo, of course, who has come to meet his fellow Trustees. You're not seriously suggesting that a Trustee caused all this mayhem?'

Connie's toes were freezing. She had lost her slippers at some point during the struggle on the beach.

'It wasn't like the other times,' she said fervently, rubbing her feet. 'I've been awake the whole time. I *know* that I didn't summon this storm.'

Evelyn, who had been standing at Connie's shoulder all this while, moved uneasily. 'With respect, this isn't the time to discuss this.' Evelyn looked to

Kinga and Kira to back her. 'They're soaked. Let's go inside before they all freeze to death.'

Mr Coddrington unfolded his arms and stepped into the centre of the circle that had formed around Connie. 'You're right,' he said with a nod at Evelyn. 'We'll have a chance to hear her excuses at the appeal: tomorrow night at the Mastersons'—a full hearing before her Chapter and the Trustees. Make sure she is there.'

Evelyn helped Connie up. 'Would you like to dry off by our fire, Eagle-Child?' she asked, extending a hand to the Native American.

Eagle-Child's piercing look made Connie feel terrible. 'No thank you, Evelyn. I will return to the Mastersons'.' His rejection of her aunt's offer seemed to Connie to be the worst thing that had happened that night: Eagle-Child had always been her friend and she had rested her hopes in him being one of her staunchest allies at her appeal.

'Fine,' said Evelyn in a disappointed tone. 'Then we'll see you all tomorrow.'

Connie sat in the kitchen in dry clothes with her hands cupped round a steaming mug of milk and honey. Mack was indulging in something stronger from a hip flask in the armchair by the fireplace. Evelyn was on her knees attempting to get a blaze started in the grate. Argand hopped into the kitchen and relieved her of the task with one quick blast of flames. Evelyn jumped back as the fire leapt into life in a billow of golden sparks. The room was silent, except for the crackle of the flames and the rasp of Argand's claws on the tiles as she skittered over to sit on Connie's toes.

'It really wasn't me,' Connie said miserably, her feet smarting as they defrosted under the warmth of the dragonet's body. 'I saw the horses from my window and I knew I had to do something about them.'

Evelyn sighed and sat down on Mack's knee. He put his arms consolingly around her. 'Are you absolutely sure of that, Connie?' she asked.

'Yes,' Connie said quickly. 'The storm started long before I went out. Ask Argand. She was asleep on my bed until the moment I got up and called out to you.' Argand's liquid gold eyes blinked trustingly up at her.

'But she was asleep,' said Mack, 'she won't make a very good witness.'

'And she'll get into trouble for being here if you do call her,' said Evelyn with a shake of her head. 'I don't mind about us others—but she's only a baby really.' Argand glared at Connie's aunt and shot out a contemptuous cloud of red sparks. 'Don't do that, Argand!' Evelyn snapped. 'As if things aren't bad enough already. The last thing we want is for the house to burn down now.'

Connie sipped her drink but put it down abruptly as it scalded her tongue. She was tired; she was cold; she wished she had never woken up. She felt buried in a landslide where everything she did made things worse.

'So no one will believe me?' Connie looked up at Evelyn. 'You don't believe me, do you?'

'I'm trying to, Connie,' Evelyn said wearily. 'But it did cross my mind that maybe my story about my aunt might've made you wonder what it would be like to summon the white horses . . . '

'I wouldn't be so stupid as to call them now, not when I know that the cliff's so dangerous!' exclaimed Connie indignantly.

'I suppose not,' said Evelyn, biting her lip. She took the hip flask from Mack and took a big swig.

'Come on, Evie,' Mack said, hugging her tight, 'give the girl a break. It was a brave thing she did drawing the horses away. It was no fun under their hooves, believe me.'

'You're right,' said Evelyn, wiping her mouth. 'Sorry, Connie. It's just all getting to me. It's like someone's after us—making everything possible go wrong.'

The back door slammed open and Gard stamped in, shaking the wreath of snow from his head. The flakes did not melt on him but stayed in every crack and crevice.

'The good news is that the cliff behind the house is stable,' he said, brushing more snow off his shoulders, 'but you've lost a fair chunk further down the beach.'

Evelyn got up to take Gard's cloak from him. 'There's a hearing tomorrow,' she said.

'That is to be expected. I know that it was no fault of Connie's that we had that storm. Her feet did not hit the ground until well after the storm had begun.'

At last, thought Connie, here was someone who did not doubt her. The relief in the room was palpable.

'Will you tell them this tomorrow?' asked Evelyn.

'Certainly.'

'But they won't believe you, will they?' said Connie pessimistically as she recalled the grim expressions of the Trustees.

'They will believe me, Universal, but they will not believe you, I fear, until the creature that created the storm is identified. Do you know?'

'It was a weather giant. I felt the ache in my head—just here.' She pressed her temples—it had gone now.

'Not Kullervo then?'

'No, I don't think so. His presence is different.'

'Then it is more important than ever to show them his mark and explain what has been happening. Prepare yourself for a rough ride. There will be those who doubt you no matter what you say, and some who reject you even if they think you are telling the truth.'

'Why?'

'Because they fear you.'

This was hard to accept but she knew he was right.

'Do you still want me to talk to the stone sprites tomorrow—I mean today?' she asked, hearing the clock in the hall strike one o'clock.

'Yes. After this storm, we must get to work on this cliff immediately.'

'OK,' Connie said with resignation. 'Well, it looks like today is shaping up to be really great. I think I'll go to bed before it gets any worse.'

*

185

The encounter with the stone sprites was even more unpleasant than she had feared. With Gard by her side, she crouched at the bottom of the cliff in the chill of the morning and bored into the cliff to find them. They wriggled out to embrace her, pale hands grasping at her wrists, greeting her as a stone-sister in their cold, still world. Their touch bit into her. They hungered for silence; they wanted the earth to return to peace. Humans were so many maggots crawling on the outside of their rocky home, digging into its crust without leave. Driven mad by the ravaging of their land, the sprites had fled deep into the ground, surfacing only occasionally to vent their spite on the warm-blooded beings that sapped the strength of the earth like parasites on a once-healthy host.

Connie was too tired to argue with the sprites; she had no energy to attempt to show them that not all humans sought to destroy.

'Please,' she pleaded, 'don't be angry with all of us. Help us by mending the rock with your strength. You're the only ones who can prevent it falling; only you can stop me being forced away from this place. They may send me somewhere where you can no longer reach me—a place where I can be of no use to you.'

Then Gard joined her in the shared bond and explained what was needed.

'Brothers, you can sense the fault-lines too—the weaknesses hammered in by wave and wind. Strengthen the rock, fill the cracks, renew the stone.'

'We will do as you ask,' the sprites said in their hungry voices. 'Your cold flesh is to our liking, Rock Dwarf. But you, Universal . . .' (the sprites increased their grip on Connie's wrists) ' . . . you should let us chill you to our temperature. Become stone.'

Connie shrank from their touch.

'I cannot live like you,' she whispered. 'Please let me go.'

The stone in the cliff creaked. For a moment, Connie thought that the sprites were going to bring it down on her head for rejecting their offer. But then the hands released their grip, leaving pale finger marks on her skin, and shrivelled back into the rock.

Connie bowed her head. Perhaps, after all, she should have accepted them. Turning to cold, inert stone would have been one way of avoiding all the problems that had piled up around her.

The encounter made Connie late for school. Col and Rat spent their English lesson looking at the door every time someone passed, thinking it would be her. They were eager to ask her about the special session of the Chapter they had been summoned to by an early morning telephone call from Dr Brock. He had told them very little, just saying that Connie's appeal was to be heard that night.

'Do you think they'll let her off?' asked Rat as they leafed through their shared copy of *The Tempest*.

'Dunno,' Col shrugged. 'I 'spect so.'

'Got to, haven't they? After what you lot discovered—and the fact that she's the only universal we've got.'

'I s'pose.' Col was feeling less certain. There was something in Dr Brock's tone that suggested all was not well.

Connie came in towards the end of the lesson looking tired and grim-faced. She sat on her own, barely listening to anything that was said.

Chair-legs scraped as the class abandoned the room for break. Col and Rat swooped on Connie and frogmarched her to a quiet bench away from the others.

'See you've got your appeal today,' Col began. 'That's good, isn't it?'

'Not really,' said Connie, frowning.

'Why not?' Col ruffled his hair and reached in his pocket for his shades as protection against the sunshine glancing off the melting snow.

'Well, you'd better wait to hear the whole story tonight. But I didn't do it, no matter what Mr Coddrington claims.'

'Didn't do what?' asked Rat eagerly.

'Raise the snowstorm last night. The Trustees caught me trying to stop the white horses bringing the cliff down on our house. Appearances aren't good.' Connie nibbled one of her short nails.

'That's bad,' said Col, whistling softly.

'So it wasn't you who made that storm then?' said Rat.

'No.'

'Oh,' he said, disappointed.

'Was that why you were late?' asked Col.

Connie shook her head and hugged her arms to her chest. 'No. I had to speak to the stone sprites for Gard. They're going to shore up the cliff for us.'

'Stone sprites?' queried Col. 'You mean those things that tried to kill my parents last year?'

'Yep—that's them. They're cold and horrible. They creep into you like icy worms trying to gnaw out your heart. I can't bring myself to like them even though they've agreed to help us.'

'So why are they?' Rat asked.

'To put me in their debt. I can help them talk to the rock dwarves and others, you see. They think I might be useful to them.'

From the knot of pupils at the doors, they saw Anneena approaching.

'Why are you all hiding over here?' she called. 'I've been looking for you for ages.'

'Oh hi, Anneena. Where's Jane?' Connie asked.

'Oh.' Anneena raised her eyebrows in an arch expression. 'I left her talking to a boy from the photography club—they've been doing a lot of that recently.'

Connie was surprised: she had missed out on so much being wrapped up in her own problems. She had not even noticed Jane's new friendship.

'So, are they going out with each other?' Rat asked with a smirk.

'As far as I can tell, they tend rather to be staying in—in the dark room.' Anneena smiled.

'Oh yeah?' said Rat.

'Oh come on, Rat. It's perfectly possible to be together a lot and just to be friends,' said Connie, defending the absent Jane.

'Yeah. You mean like you and Col?' Rat suggested.

Col gave him a warning look—Rat enjoyed needling him about Captain Graves's suspicions. He could put up with it as long as Connie didn't catch on.

'Exactly. Just good friends,' said Connie, wondering why Rat laughed.

Concerned to create a positive first impression, Connie, Evelyn, Mack, and Gard arrived early for the appeal. Shirley Masterson met them in the yard, muffled up in a thick fur-lined coat and carrying a flashlight.

'Here already then? Dad's asked me to show Society members into the kitchen but I suppose she should go into the barn,' Shirley said, giving Connie a cold look. 'The rest of you can go on up to the house if you like.'

'No thanks. We're sticking with Connie,' said Evelyn, gripping Connie's forearm.

'You know the way, I suppose,' said Shirley, flashing the torch towards the big double-doors to their right.

'We do,' said Evelyn. She pulled Connie after her. 'What a cow!' she muttered fiercely. Connie said nothing, too low already to be bothered by Shirley.

As the first to arrive they found the barn in darkness. It took them some time to locate the light-switch on one of the wooden beams. Raw white light hit their eyes as the strip-light in the centre of the roof stuttered on. The room had been prepared for the meeting. At one end were ranged four chairs and space for a dragon, a unicorn, and Storm-Bird. Behind them, hay-bales had been piled in a terrace to accommodate a large audience. At the other end, a single wooden chair was set facing the spectators.

'We can't have that!' said Mack at once. He began hefting hay-bales over to Connie's side, creating a sofa of three bales for them. He hid the hard chair in the shadows.

'Good idea,' said Evelyn, 'let's bring some more.' Together they dragged six hay-bales and arranged them in a horseshoe. Gard kicked them into place. 'Now you sit there,' said Evelyn, pointing to the centre, 'and we'll sit around you.'

Connie sank down on the middle bale, comforted by having her supporters with her. They waited. Beasts and beings began to arrive. Dr Brock and Argot were amongst the first. Taking one look at the arrangement of the room, they both immediately turned to sit at Connie's end, Argot curling his tail right round the back of the horseshoe of bales. Dr Brock smiled encouragingly at Connie.

'Good work last night, Connie,' he said loudly, his voice carrying to the people sitting opposite, some of the Chartmouth members that Connie did not know very well.

Captain Graves came in with Mr Masterson. Glancing towards Connie and muttering together, they turned to take a seat on the front of the terrace.

'It's like bride or groom,' grinned Mack at Connie, referring to the tradition at a wedding where the guests sit on different sides. She couldn't even smile in response.

Rat came in and absent-mindedly sat in the first space available on the terrace. He then looked up and realized what was happening. Clambering over Mr Masterson as he jumped to the floor, he swiftly crossed to Connie's side.

'You twit, Rat,' said Mack, ruffling the boy's hair and pulling him onto the seat next to him.

'Twit yourself, mate,' said Rat cheerfully. 'All right, Connie?'

'I'm OK,' she replied.

Argand flew in, swooping once round the heads of all present, croaking rudely at the people sitting on the terrace, before landing at Connie's feet. Then Jessica Moss slipped into the barn, accompanied by Arran. Greeting Connie, they both took places on her right. Erik Ulvsen entered in a swirl of icy air. He strode over to the universal's side, bowed to the girl he thought of as his pack leader, and then took a seat at the end of her row.

Nearly all places in the barn were now occupied, except for the chairs facing Connie. Finally the Trustees filed in, led by Mr Coddrington. He looked with dismay at the change to his seating arrangements and seemed to be on the point of protesting. Kinga, however, had walked past him and taken a place in

192

the middle. Not wishing to lose a prime position for himself, he hurried after her and sat down. Storm-Bird flew in to perch on a sack of fertilizer placed there for its comfort. Morjik and Windfoal settled themselves at either end of the row. As for the weather giant, he could not fit inside but, from the pressure building in her temples, Connie could sense his presence gathering in the yard. A pillar of shifting cloud swirled outside the door, blotting out the stars.

'Right, close the doors. I think we are all present and correct,' said Mr Coddrington, rubbing his hands together. He for one seemed to be relishing the meeting ahead. 'We should make a start. Will the former Society member stand forward.'

Trembling, Connie got to her feet. But before another word could be said, the door banged wide open to let in four late-comers.

'Sorry we're late,' Mrs Clamworthy apologized, unwrapping her scarf. 'I don't like driving on these icy roads. Icefen, you should really keep your breath to yourself!'

The frost wolf padded in behind, licking his lips.

Col guided his grandmother on one side, Skylark on the other in case she slipped. He saw that all eyes, including those of Captain Graves, were fixed on them, wondering which way they would go. Mrs Clamworthy looked quickly from Mr Coddrington, to Connie, to the seating arrangements.

'Oh good,' she said lightly, 'I see you've saved us some space over there.'

Walking right across the centre of the room, she led Col, Skylark, and the wolf to the hay-bales on

Connie's left and squeezed in next to Mack. Glancing across at his mentor as he sat down, Col saw Captain Graves frown.

'As I was saying,' said Mr Coddrington testily. 'Now that we're all comfortable—'

'Quite comfortable, thank you, Ivor,' trilled Mrs Clamworthy, interrupting him again.

'Then we shall start.' Mr Coddrington's pleasure at the proceedings had evaporated to be replaced by annoyance at the insubordination of so many members. His tone was waspish. 'Stand forward, Connie Lionheart.'

14

Defence

Connie took a small step forward, her hand resting on Argand's upturned head for comfort. Never one to seek the limelight, this was her worst nightmare: to be standing in front of all these people with everyone's eyes on her.

'Connie Lionheart, you lodged an appeal against your expulsion. The purpose of this meeting is to decide whether the grounds for expulsion will be upheld,' said Mr Coddrington, regaining his stride once more. His gaze slid over Connie and her friends to the people clustered on the terraces either side of him. 'The grounds are as follows: one, on at least two occasions, you did wilfully and recklessly summon storms that inflicted extensive damage on this locality; two, you did wilfully and recklessly attempt to harm, and nearly caused the death of three Society members; three, you did slander a Trustee of the Society, accusing him of being in league with our enemy, Kullervo . . .'

Dr Brock raised his hand. Kinga jerked Mr Coddrington's sleeve to draw his attention to the intervention.

'Yes?' said Mr Coddrington, impatient to get on.

Dr Brock got to his feet. 'As I remember, Ivor, Connie did not accuse you of being in league with Kullervo; she merely said you were doing his work for him by ousting her from the Society. You must admit, there is a difference. One might even say, she had a point.'

'Hear, hear!' said Mack loudly.

Connie felt a flood of gratitude to her friend, though if the truth were known she had meant her words rather in the sense Mr Coddrington described, and not in Dr Brock's more favourable construction. She was not, however, about to admit this.

Mr Coddrington tugged at his tight shirt collar uncomfortably. 'Of course she doesn't have a point. Whatever can you mean?'

'Only that isolating Connie is the very thing Kullervo would want. It would make her much more vulnerable to his attack.' Dr Brock sat down but looked hard at Kinga and then at Morjik over the top of his spectacles. 'Indeed, I think you'll find he's already been testing her defences.'

'Well, never mind that,' snapped Mr Coddrington. 'There is enough to be going on with in the first two charges. And you cannot deny, Francis, that whatever Miss Lionheart meant, she was unforgivably rude to a Trustee?'

'Rude, yes, but not unforgivably so, I hope,' replied Dr Brock.

Mr Coddrington cleared his throat to call for silence as a buzz of voices broke out around him. 'I have also, on the instructions of my fellow Trustees, to add to our considerations a fourth ground— namely, the storm she summoned yesterday, placing in jeopardy her own life and that of two others who courageously went to her rescue.'

Connie shook her head, bursting to be allowed an opportunity to deny this charge of which she knew she was completely innocent, but Mr Coddrington had not finished. Desperately, she looked to Kira, to Kinga, to Eagle-Child but they all had their eyes on Mr Coddrington and were avoiding her gaze. She felt out for Morjik, Windfoal, and Storm-Bird but they did not answer her call, shutting themselves away from her.

'Now, let us get down to business,' said Mr Coddrington, cracking his knuckles. 'Connie Lionheart, did you, or did you not, summon the storms in November and December?'

'I did,' she said. There was a gasp from the people in the terrace behind the Trustees. 'But . . .'

'So you admit the charge?' he pressed gleefully.

'Yes. But it wasn't wilful, or whatever you said. It wasn't . . .'

'I've heard all this before,' said Mr Coddrington in a bored tone of voice, rolling his eyes to the ceiling. 'You are going to tell us "it wasn't like that" but then you'll say you can't explain it.'

Kinga stood up. 'With respect, Ivor, *you* may have heard it before, but *we* have not. We have come all the way from Japan to hear this explanation.'

197

'Of course, Kinga,' he said obsequiously, realizing that he had made a strategic error in forgetting that he was no longer the only Trustee present, 'but you'll find the universal's excuses wear thin very rapidly.'

'Let us judge that for ourselves,' said Kinga. 'Connie, please continue.' The dragon companion turned back to Connie, expecting her to pick up her narrative, but saw instead that, during this short exchange, a change had come over the universal: her skin seemed to be shining with a faint silvery light; her eyes were fixed upon the barn door. 'Connie, are you listening?'

With difficulty, Connie dragged her eyes back to Kinga and said hoarsely: 'There are hundreds of creatures out there. They're all trying to bond with me. They're waiting to come in.'

'Creatures?' said Kinga bewildered. 'All Society members are welcome to be present at this hearing. Why aren't they coming in? Let them in, someone.'

Mr Masterson jumped to his feet and threw open the doors. He was forced back as a torrent of creatures poured into the room: misshapen rock dwarves, hobbling wood sprites, brown-oozing water sprites, and bringing up the rear, a minotaur with one blind eye. Many of the members gave cries of distress as injured beasts and beings from their companies brushed past them. The creatures swirled into the centre of the barn, flinching in the bright light and shielding their eyes, before moving to occupy the shadows behind the horseshoe of bales. Connie's side now far out-numbered the members sitting with the Trustees.

'Who are all these creatures?' asked Kinga, looking to Connie for an explanation.

The minotaur stomped into the centre of the room and glared at Kinga, his breath snorting from his distended nostrils. 'They are friends of the universal,' he growled, 'and I am the universal's sentinel.'

A ghost of a smile flickered across Eagle-Child's lips and for the first time he met Connie's gaze and nodded slightly in her direction.

'Are you Society members?' rapped out Mr Coddrington, consulting a sheaf of paper he held in his hand. 'I don't remember there being a minotaur in Devon.'

The minotaur threw back his head and gave a bellow of bitter laughter. 'No, we are not on your lists, Trustee. We have fallen off all lists. We are the creatures that live beneath the regard of the Society, the ones you with your systems and procedures would prefer to forget. We are the casualties of the war mankind is waging with the earth.'

Mr Coddrington quickly reached the conclusion that it would not enhance his reputation in the Society if he were seen to eject a crowd of disabled veterans. He put down his papers and took a step towards Sentinel, holding out a welcoming hand. His smile was insincere.

'In that case, it is time we did take notice. I am sure the Society will be able to help, but that must be dealt with later, because now we are engaged in a most serious—'

Sentinel ignored the outstretched hand. 'You cannot help us. Your Society members have done enough. I could introduce you to creatures who are only here because of him and his mistakes.' The minotaur raised an accusing finger and pointed at Mr Masterson and then at the bag of fertilizer on which Storm-Bird was perched.

The farmer quailed. The accusation evidently rang true with him immediately. 'I'm sorry about that. I reported the error to the environmental officers . . . I've tried to clean up . . .' Mr Masterson blustered.

'So you are seeking compensation?' asked Mr Coddrington. 'I think we have a fund for relocation—'

'You cannot compensate us,' growled Sentinel, 'but the universal can.'

There was an awkward silence. Kinga, her face stern, took one look at the newest Trustee and realized he did not know what to do next. She stepped forward to take the proceedings under her direction before they disintegrated further.

'As you are Connie's friend,' she said to the minotaur, 'perhaps you would like to take a seat with her? We would like to hear more about your case, of course, but whether or not the universal will be able to help you by using her powers can only be decided after we have ruled on the matter before us. It may be that she is too dangerous to be of any help to you and we will have to find another way to assist you all.'

Mr Coddrington nodded eagerly, endorsing his colleague's words with enthusiasm. 'That's right. It's as I said: now is not the time.'

The minotaur stood his ground and lowered his horns towards the row of Trustees. He pawed the floor with his right foot. Connie knew he was contemplating charging them to end the debate by force.

'Sentinel!' Connie said sharply. 'No, don't do that! It won't help me. Come stand by me, please!'

He grunted, hunching forward.

'Please!' Connie entreated.

Reluctantly, the minotaur turned his back and stalked proudly to her side, taking up position at her shoulder, arms folded across his broad chest.

Kinga gave Connie a grateful nod. 'Thank you, Connie. Let us return to your explanation.'

Heartened by the presence of her bodyguard and the ranks of supporters clustered behind her, Connie found her voice was steady and clear when she spoke again.

'What I'm going to say may be difficult to believe,' she began, 'but others can back up my story. They know I'm telling the truth. I think it all goes back to what happened in Mallins Wood. It seems that . . . that . . .' (she closed her eyes, wishing she did not have to say these next words) 'that Kullervo has left the mark of his companionship within me.' There was a murmur from the terraces and the hum of the shape-shifter's name being repeated by many mouths. 'It gives him access to me when I am asleep or' (she opened her eyes to cast a quick look at Col, remembering how she had nearly killed him) 'or when I'm feeling very angry.'

Col did not flinch but gave her an encouraging nod.

'And what happens then?' coaxed Kinga.

'I'm not sure but I think I assume Kullervo's powers. I become a channel for his urge to create havoc and chaos.'

'In that case,' said Kira, the unicorn companion, casting her orange kikoi over her shoulder as she rose to her feet, 'why are we all still here? I thought that if you unleashed Kullervo's power on us all, we'd be swept away?'

Connie nodded. 'That's what he once told me. But I think somehow I've not let it reach that point. I seem to have been controlling what I did—I suppose I've just been "playing" with the power. And both times I have been stopped by an encounter with another creature before things went too far.'

Kira, Kinga, and Eagle-Child looked at each other in wonder. Mr Coddrington, however, was incandescent.

'And what, pray, is your proof of all this?' he snapped.

Gard got to his feet. Even upright he only came to the waist of the minotaur. 'We have seen it— Sentinel, Argot, Dr Brock, Skylark, Col, and I. We entered her mind and saw the mark.'

'What! She let all these mythical creatures encounter her—blatantly flouting the rules banning further association! This has gone much further than even I suspected!' Mr Coddrington exclaimed. 'She's dangerous and you encourage her, Rock Dwarf!'

Col, sitting beside his grandmother, swallowed hard as he saw Captain Graves rap his cane into his palm and look angrily across at his pupil. He wondered if he was about to be permanently grounded.

'Do not be a fool, Companion to Weather Giants,' said Gard with great authority, needing no extra inches to make Mr Coddrington cower before him. 'We had to find out the truth—something you would never have done.'

Kira Okona and Windfoal crossed the floor to stand by Connie. 'So she can't be held responsible for what has happened?' Kira put her arm around Connie's shoulder.

'No,' said Gard firmly. 'He has been merely waiting for an opportunity to break through.'

Mr Coddrington ran his hand through his hair, aghast at the defection of two of the Trustees. 'It is worse than I feared!' he said, his voice becoming shrill. 'The girl's a ticking bomb. What evidence have we that she isn't colluding with him and letting him use her? We only have her word for it. I've never heard the like of it before.'

'Oh yes, you have,' said Mack gruffly, pushing Col forward. 'It happened to Col, didn't it? Go on: tell him.'

Col looked once at Connie and then turned to face the Trustees. 'Kullervo can force his way into you if he wants,' he said, keeping his eyes on Kinga as he guessed she was nearly persuaded, 'but he uses what's in you. In me, he found I liked fighting and used that, pushing it a little further each time until I became hardened to it and enjoyed bloodshed. In Connie, I suppose he's found a desire to play with her power. Let's hope he doesn't get the chance to

203

push it any further. I've been on the receiving end of one of her thunderbolts and that was enough.'

Kinga smiled and Morjik rumbled, giving vent to a subterranean chuckle.

'So!' spluttered Mr Coddrington. 'She's an open door for Kullervo and you are proposing we let her back into the Society!'

'We have the matter contained,' said Gard, creaking ominously as he fingered his mallet. He looked as if he would like to deploy it on the Trustee's head. 'We have placed a guard on Connie. While she is bonded with another, it appears that Kullervo finds it difficult to break through.'

'Contained, you say!' squealed Mr Coddrington. 'So, in that case, what was last night all about?'

'I can vouch for the fact that Connie was not outside until the storm was far advanced,' said Gard calmly.

'But perhaps she can summon storms from inside. Who knows what a universal can do?' Mr Coddrington's slicked-back hair fell over his eyes as his hand sliced the air, finger pointing at Connie.

She steeled herself to confront him, reluctantly deciding she must speak again. 'No one knows, not even me. But I do know I didn't summon that storm. I was on the beach to stop the white horses crashing into the cliff. I suppose either you believe me, or you don't. It's my word against what you thought you saw.'

Storm-Bird gave a shrill whistle from its perch and Eagle-Child moved in his cat-like prowl to stand before Connie. He rested a hand on her shoulder

204

and looked into her eyes. 'I'm sorry I doubted you, Universal,' he said. He dropped his hand and took his place by the minotaur, a second bodyguard with arms folded across his chest.

Morjik let out a plume of white smoke which drifted across the space between him and Connie, wreathing her in his warm breath.

Kinga turned to Mr Coddrington. 'I think I speak for the other Trustees when I say that we feel the grounds for Connie's expulsion no longer look so firm. We will need to see this mark for ourselves, of course, but it seems to me that we should reinstate her fully if we are satisfied by what this reveals.'

There was an angry murmuring from some of the people on the terrace. Captain Graves raised his hand.

'Yes?' asked Kinga.

'Trustee, you may speak for the Trustees, but I know I speak for many of us here in the Chartmouth Chapter when I say that we have nothing against Connie personally but we are concerned that you are not doing enough to ensure the safety of others. The universal is dangerous. Mr Coddrington called her a ticking bomb; well, I would just like to point out that she has already gone off twice. How many more incidents will it take before someone gets killed?'

Kinga nodded her head gravely and looked over to Morjik. The dragon flickered his tongue into the air; his fiery eyes blinked once.

'We must be mindful of this, of course,' said Kinga, 'but I am of the opinion—an opinion which I see her friends share—that we can better help Connie if she

205

is within the Society. She would be more dangerous outside.'

Captain Graves inclined his head. 'I take your point, Trustee, but surely she must not be allowed to continue without supervision? Who knows what the exercise of her powers will lead to?'

'Yes, yes!' said Mr Coddrington, grasping at straws as he saw his victory fast disappearing. 'She must be kept under lock and key until this matter is settled, one way or another.'

'No!' said Gard angrily, his eyes beginning to blaze with red fire as if the coal from which he was made had ignited. 'She is not a criminal, Coddrington! Surround her with her friends, by all means, but stop persecuting her just because she has gifts that you do not understand.'

Mr Coddrington took a step towards the rock dwarf. Gard raised his mallet.

'Enough!' Kinga ordered, stepping between them. 'I propose that Connie be reinstated to the Society on the condition that she shows us Kullervo's mark. Secondly, that the guard be continued, but in a way that allows her to carry on with her ordinary life. Other encounters or exercise of the universal's power should be restricted to only that which is essential to the investigation into her condition. This should continue until such time as we are satisfied that she does not pose a threat to herself or others. Do my colleagues agree?' Kinga's eagle-bright eyes swept around the circle of her fellow Trustees. 'If I read this rightly, the proposal is carried six votes to two.'

Mr Coddrington crumpled up his papers in disgust.

Kinga felt in her pocket and held out four badges.

'Connie, you are back in,' she concluded, tipping the badges onto the universal's hand. They lay on Connie's palm: crystal, wings, horse, and lizard. 'Welcome home!'

15
Dip with the Selkies

Connie did not feel much like celebrating, despite Rat's best efforts to involve her in the impromptu party at Shaker Row. Many of her friends were there and she was sincerely pleased to see their relieved, happy faces, but she could not forget that she still had to let the Trustees see Kullervo's mark.

'Are you going to go swimming with the seal boy?' asked Rat as he watched the sleek-haired selkie, Arran, drape his arm around his companion's shoulder, his nose twitching as someone offered him a tuna sandwich. 'Jessica's off for a dip with him. It'll be amazing to see him transform into a seal!'

'No thanks,' said Connie, grabbing a handful of peanuts from the bowl on the dresser, 'I've had enough of the sea for the moment.'

Dr Brock, who was passing with a glass of champagne clutched in one hand, added: 'You forget, Rat, that Connie's not supposed to go encountering creatures unless absolutely necessary.'

Rat shrugged. 'That wouldn't stop me. Selkies sound really cool.'

'Quite. That's why we all have to thank our lucky stars that it's Connie, and not you, who's the universal,' Dr Brock said caustically before going to join Gard by the fire. Rat grinned at Connie and wandered over to Jessica to angle for an introduction to Arran.

Connie was surprised to see that Col was also watching Jessica and the selkie but with a distinctly jealous look in his eyes.

'What's up, Col?' she asked softly. 'You don't look too happy.'

'No,' said Col, tearing his eyes away from the couple who were now laughing with Rat. 'I'm pleased, of course, about the appeal, but it's just that . . . well, I'm still grounded. I thought Captain Graves might let me off now you're reinstated but he said I had to learn a lesson about rules and that what happened to you didn't count.'

'Oh,' she said, shaking her head sadly, 'I'm really sorry.'

Now that Col had started he found it a relief to let all his woes tumble out. 'He told me he was thinking of extending the punishment after hearing about our little expedition with Sentinel. He said I'd be lucky to get away with just a month.' Col snapped a breadstick into smaller and smaller pieces, thinking of what he would like to do to his mentor's cane. 'Then Skylark told him to take a running jump and said we'd fly together whatever the old windbag said, which means he's now in trouble too. He'll probably also be grounded and that'll be much worse for him than it is for me.'

'Ah.'

'But at least it means that no one else gets to ride him, so I can't help feeling happy about that, but then I feel guilty for feeling happy, do you understand?'

Connie nodded, hiding a smile.

'And don't say "it's only a month" like Gran does, because flying with Skylark is everything to me.'

'I won't, I promise.'

Col suddenly remembered to whom he was talking. 'I'm so sorry, Connie. Here I am going on about this when you've got so much more to worry about!'

'No, it's fine—really, it's fine. It's good to hear other people's problems: it helps take your mind off your own.'

'Yeah,' said Col, giving her a swift one-armed hug, 'you're right.'

'Er . . . hem!' Rat had returned and was standing behind Col. 'Not interrupting anything, I hope?'

'Nope,' said Col, quickly moving away from Connie.

'Good, because I wanted to tell Connie that I've done it—I'm going swimming with a changeling creature—now!'

'You're mad!' laughed Connie. 'It's January! Only a Sea Snake could survive out there.'

'What's a bit of cold water when you have a chance to take a dip with a selkie?' said Rat over his shoulder, following Jessica and her companion out of the door.

Rat missed school for the next few days. He was suffering from hypothermia, according to his mother. She was so angry with him for having gone swimming at midnight that she was refusing to let anyone in to see him. Even Mack could not win her round when he brought Col over for a visit.

'The idiot boy went for a swim in nothing but a pair of pants!' She waved her arms in the direction of the upstairs bedroom where the feverish Rat was cloistered. 'Of course I'm not letting anyone see him! No sympathy and grapes for him! He's a no-good waste of space like his father! Even a squid has more brains than him!'

'Oh, come on, Siobhan,' interrupted Mack, 'some squids I know are very intelligent.'

Siobhan gave him a funny look. 'You're cracked yourself, Mack Clamworthy. It was probably you who gave him the idea—running off to the beach half-cut at your party from what I hear.'

'You know me, Siobhan,' said Mack, giving her a wink, 'I like to live on the edge.'

'Ha!' Mrs Ratcliff laughed scornfully, throwing back her mop of red hair. 'You're well over the edge, Mack, but I don't want you dragging my son after you.'

'I had nothing to do with his swim the other night, I swear,' said Mack hurriedly, thumping his hand to his chest. 'Col, you tell her.'

Col shook his head. 'He didn't. It was Jessica.'

'So, it was a girl, was it!' she crowed. 'Wait till I tell him what I think of him chasing the girls. Trying to impress her, I've no doubt.'

'Er . . . it wasn't . . . ' said Col, aware he had unwittingly landed Rat in more trouble. But Mrs Ratcliff was under full sail and took no heed of his attempt to correct her.

'But how he thinks a scrawny thing like him, all covered in goosebumps, will impress a girl, I don't know. You'd better go,' she said, going back into the cottage, 'as you're wasting your time here. Don't worry—I'll boot him back to school as soon as he's well enough to stand. There are no malingerers in my house.'

Pausing by the bike to put on their helmets, Mack and Col looked at each other and grimaced.

'Sounds bad, doesn't it?' said Col.

'Oh, he'll be all right,' said Mack, buckling his strap under his chin. 'She'll look after him, despite all that sound and fury.'

'I s'pose,' said Col. He turned to take in the progress being made on the wind farm. Six tall white masts were standing erect in the field, towering over the pine plantation behind them like outsize weeds. A crane loomed over the plots for the final two, which were lying in pieces at its feet. This part of Dartmoor would soon be out of bounds for the pegasi. 'Almost finished then?'

'Yeah,' said Mack. 'And now that diplomatic relations have been restored between Evie and Mr Masterson, we've been invited to the opening this

212

weekend.' He fired up the bike. 'Come on, mate, I haven't got all day.'

Col climbed on behind his father and put his arms around his waist. Thrown back by the kick of the bike as it surged away, he tightened his grip. Col watched the masts disappear behind the hedges. The last thing he saw before the bike turned a corner was their outstretched blades appealing like semaphore signals to the sky. He wondered if they were showing the way to the future, or merely waving a last farewell before humankind irreparably damaged the world that had sustained its population for aeons. Despite his misgivings, he hoped the wind farm was a sign of a more careful humanity, something the Society could use to prove to the creatures tempted to go over to Kullervo that mankind could change, but he wasn't convinced that it was enough.

At breakfast on Friday morning, Evelyn burst into the kitchen and threw a letter at Mack's chest. Gard, who had been slumbering by the fire, woke with a start.

'Look!' she cried. 'They've not taken any notice of my letters! They've not even bothered to come and re-investigate the cliff after all the trouble Gard and Connie have taken getting the stone sprites to help!'

Mack put down his coffee cup and read the letter. As he did so, he rose to his feet, his free hand clenched, and swore colourfully.

'They won't,' he said when he reached the end. 'They can't!'

'Oh yes, they will and they can!' Evelyn said, kicking the back door in her frustration.

Watching this performance without fully understanding what was behind it, Connie stretched out her hand for the letter.

'Can I read that?' she asked. Evelyn and Mack exchanged a glance.

'You'd better not,' Evelyn said, whisking the letter away from Mack and putting it back in its envelope.

'Why not?'

'Well, you've got a big day ahead taking the Trustees to see the mark. You don't need anything else to worry about.'

'But that makes it worse!' said Connie. 'I'm going to think all sorts of terrible things if you don't tell me what's going on.'

'She is right,' said Gard. 'You had better tell us what is in that letter.'

'OK,' said Evelyn with a sigh and sitting down at the table. 'The council wants us to leave.'

'Leave?' gasped Connie.

Evelyn nodded.

'But they can't—not now the stone sprites have helped us!'

'I'm sorry, but that doesn't wash with the council. We've got to get them back here somehow to look at it again. But I don't know how we are going to persuade them. We'll need a miracle—something really dramatic—to make them think again.'

*

214

It was a crisp cloudless night as Connie, Col, Mack and Evelyn got ready to meet the Trustees at the mines.

Stepping out into the darkness, Evelyn linked arms with Connie. She could feel her niece shivering with a combination of cold and nerves.

'I'm sure it'll be fine,' she said softly as Mack closed the back door. 'Just do as they ask and you'll be OK.'

'I s'pose,' said Connie miserably. 'But it's not easy, you know.'

'I imagine it's very odd, having people inside you, prying into all corners.'

'Yes, but the most difficult thing's not interfering. I've discovered that my mind's a very weird place.'

'Well, I'm sure the Trustees won't do anything to provoke you. All they want to do is see this mark.'

The Trustees were waiting with Sentinel at the entrance to the mine. Morjik and Kinga had lit a fire, bathing the dell with rich orange light. As Connie approached, she noticed that the shadows of bird, dragon, unicorn, and minotaur were flickering on the rock face behind them, casting elongated imprints of themselves like the pictures on her mental wall of encounters.

'Connie, welcome,' said Kinga, showing her to a seat by Sentinel. Evelyn, Col, and Mack took their places on a stone slab behind the circle of Trustees. 'We're just waiting for Ivor Coddrington: he's summoning Hoo.'

Connie gulped. 'I didn't know they were coming too.' She should have realized this before, she thought, angry with herself. She had given herself no time to prepare.

'Of course,' said Kinga. 'All the Trustees must be present.'

'But I've never encountered a weather giant before. I'm not sure what'll happen. Sustaining so many bonds at once is difficult enough . . .' The last thing she wanted was Mr Coddrington wandering about in her mind.

Kinga frowned. 'We understand, but we all need to see the proof—that includes them, I'm afraid.'

A twig snapped on the path beyond the light cast by the fire.

'Of course it does,' said Mr Coddrington as he emerged from the darkness. Connie sensed a presence behind him; dark cloud obscured the stars where the giant stood between them and the sky. 'We insist that we go ahead as agreed. I will not be satisfied unless I see this supposed mark for myself.'

Connie seethed. Supposed mark? Anyone would think to hear him speak that she had been making it all up. She had to try once more to make herself understood to Kinga.

'You see, it's just that I find it difficult to control things if I'm feeling upset.'

The minotaur grunted with understanding.

'If you want to be in the Society, you'll have to learn to do as you're told,' said Mr Coddrington tartly.

Storm-Bird gave an angry squawk and pecked at the ground right by Mr Coddrington's feet, making him jump back in alarm.

'Sorry, just spotted a worm,' said Eagle-Child, giving the weather giant companion a strange look.

'Do your best, Connie,' said Kinga as she cast a warning glance at the Native American and his companion. 'We can ask no more of you.'

Connie nodded reluctantly.

'Are you ready?' asked Kinga.

'Yes,' Connie replied, trying to focus her mind and calm her emotions.

Sentinel took her gently by the shoulders and looked round at the Trustees. 'The paths of the mind are never the same twice,' he warned them. 'It will be like starting anew. Follow me. Do nothing to provoke our host. Touch nothing.' With that he closed his eyes and Connie immediately saw his shape reappear at the door to her mind. He was swiftly joined by Storm-Bird, Morjik, and Windfoal, and shortly after by their companions.

'Where are Ivor and Hoo?' asked Kinga. Her shadow-self paced up and down looking into the dark. Reluctantly Connie reached out to Hoo, heading for the source of the buzzing in her head that she always experienced in the presence of weather giants. A cold fist advanced to meet her. Uncurling, the shadow-Ivor stepped out beside the other Trustees. The giant himself swirled around them, taking no distinct shape but shifting like storm-driven clouds.

'Let us begin,' said Sentinel, stepping through the portal.

The last time Sentinel had visited the universal's mind, it had been a bewildering but not a hostile place. This time, as soon as he entered, a strong current of air started blowing against him, trying to drive him back the way he had come. He said nothing, but bent his head against the wind. Connie watched with dismay, wondering how she could help him. It seemed that part of her was in rebellion against her conscious self. The shadow-Morjik extended his wings slightly to shield his companion; Kira clung on to Windfoal's neck. Eagle-Child and Storm-Bird followed close behind, taking advantage of the shelter the dragon was providing. Mr Coddrington stumbled along at the rear, wreathed in the rags of mist of his companion. Watching them, Connie realized that her mind was trying to disperse the weather giant and evict his companion. She had to take action or the encounter would be over before it even started. Concentrating hard, she sent a counter-current to blow from behind the Trustees. With a great effort, she forced the gale back down the corridor and mentally slammed a door against it. The Trustees were now able to make swifter progress.

'This way!' said Sentinel, showing the Trustees a broad flight of steps. With confident leaps, he bounded down two at a time, closely followed by Eagle-Child. Storm-Bird and Morjik half-stepped, half-glided down the stairs. Kira dismounted to lead Windfoal and the unicorn trotted gingerly down one stair at a time. But when Mr Coddrington put his foot on the first ledge, the stairs suddenly disappeared beneath him, becoming as smooth as a slide. His feet gave way and he skidded, suit jacket flying out behind him, all the way to the bottom. When he stood up, the seat of his trousers had ripped, revealing a glimpse of red and white underpants, vivid against his shadow-body. A muffled noise echoed around the corridors like a distant audience laughing. He pulled his jacket low over the tear and muttered angrily to Sentinel:

'Tell her to behave, can't you!'

Sentinel merely glowered at him.

'She did warn us,' said Kinga with a smile. 'You are lucky it wasn't any worse.'

'She's doing it on purpose!' he protested. 'It's all a part with her outrageous conduct!'

There was a loud crack and the rock at Mr Coddrington's feet split open, separating him from the others by a deep fissure.

'I would not say any more, if I were you,' said Eagle-Child quietly, holding out a hand to help Mr Coddrington jump across the chasm. 'You are on her territory now. It is always unwise to insult your host, never more so than when you are at the mercy of her mood.'

Mr Coddrington glanced nervously behind him. A lick of fire leapt out of the fissure and darted up the walls as if feeling out for him. He moved closer to the American.

'Of course, you're right,' he said. 'Let us get this over with before she has the chance to do anything else.'

Sentinel led his party through the network of dark corridors. Passageways branched off left and right, but Sentinel was certain of his path and did not falter. But then, turning a corner, he came to an abrupt stop. Before him stretched a vast expanse of black water: an underground lake.

'As I said,' he growled, 'each visit reveals something new.' He tested the water with his hoof, sending ripples out across the mirror-like surface.

'Is it deep?' asked Kira. 'Will Windfoal be able to wade across?'

'That depends on the universal,' said the minotaur. He took a step into the lake and laughed. 'Look, it only reaches my ankle! She is letting us through.'

The others followed him—Morjik and Storm-Bird choosing to fly rather than wet their feet. Mr Coddrington, however, paused by the bank as the weather giant swirled over the water like early morning mist.

'Are you sure it's safe?' he called to the minotaur.

'No, I am not sure,' Sentinel replied, wading on resolutely, the water gurgling around his knees.

Undecided, Mr Coddrington hovered on the bank until he saw the minotaur get out safely on the far side. He then took a step forward—and disappeared below the surface of the water to emerge spluttering and gasping seconds later.

'I can't touch the bottom!' he shouted.

'Then you'll have to swim,' replied the minotaur with a shrug, turning his back on the struggling man.

Mr Coddrington did an ungainly breaststroke across the icy lake and pulled himself out on the far side, dripping like a water rat. He seemed on the point of saying something but, after a warning look from Eagle-Child, thought better of it.

'How much further?' asked the shadow Mr Coddrington petulantly, his feet squelching in his sodden shoes.

'As far as she wants,' said the minotaur. 'We could be there in minutes, or be here for hours.'

The party walked on, scrambling over rock falls, climbing shale slopes, dropping down steep inclines and wading across streams that chattered across their path.

'I do not think she wants us to reach our destination,' said Eagle-Child calmly, looking around a glittering domed chamber that they had already passed through three times.

'Come on, Connie,' said Kinga under her breath. 'Let us in.'

A draught blew out their torches, plunging them into darkness. The Trustees stood in silence, wondering what to do next: they could not proceed without light but their host seemed unwilling to allow them any. Then, with a long, slow creak, a door swung open directly in front of them where there had been no door before. A red light flickered around its edge, broadening into a great strip on the floor at their feet.

'We are here,' cried Sentinel, rushing forward. He stepped into the cavern of the cave paintings, finding that this time it was lit with many torches in brackets along the walls. The paintings stretched as far as the eye could see in both directions, but still at the centre loomed the black mark of Kullervo. The

Trustees followed him, the weather giant swirling to assume his normal shape now that there was room to accommodate his great size.

But there was another difference to the cavern on this visit. Sentinel held up his hand to stop them hurrying forward for he had noticed a small figure with a mane of black hair, dressed in white, sitting on the floor in front of the wall, staring fixedly at Kullervo's mark.

'The universal is here,' he said softly. 'Do not disturb her.'

The Trustees tiptoed quietly around the little figure. Kira knelt beside her and gazed into the child's expressionless face, with its unblinking eyes.

'Why is she here?' Kira whispered to the minotaur. 'I thought this was all her—the corridors, the chambers, everything.'

'That is so, but the mind has the power to contemplate itself,' he said. 'None of us are simple. We have many selves.'

Connie, watching all this from her bird's eye view of the multiple bonds, was suddenly very afraid. She was afraid of the cold, still child staring at the mark, recognizing her as the part of herself that was dangerous—deadly dangerous. A rumble like an earth tremor ran through the cavern, bringing tiny pieces of rock down upon the heads of the Trustees. She was tempted to end the encounter there and then. They had seen the mark, hadn't they? Surely they should be satisfied with that?

The child rose to her feet and spoke: 'Leave now,'

she said in a dull voice, eyes still on the wall in front. 'She wants you to leave now.'

The Trustees looked at each other. Kinga approached the child cautiously.

'We need a few more minutes. We have to look at the mark. We've come all this way: surely a little more time will not hurt?'

The child did not reply so Kinga turned back to the others.

'We'd better make this swift. We've outstayed our welcome.' She strode towards the blot on the wall. 'Is it an opening or is it merely a black mark?' she asked Sentinel as she stood as close as she dared to the wall.

'I do not know,' said the minotaur, 'but the companion to pegasi said he could hear a voice and feel a breeze coming out of it.'

Kinga stood still and listened. 'Yes, there does seem to be a faint noise, like the wash of the sea on the shore,' she said.

The other Trustees crowded around her, the weather giant standing behind them, a shadowy barrier between them and the torchlight.

'What does it mean?' asked Kira, looking to Windfoal. The unicorn shook her mane uneasily.

'It's quite clear to me,' said Mr Coddrington sharply. 'It means that the universal has been irreparably damaged by Kullervo. She is his now.'

The cavern shook and a large fragment of rock fell from the ceiling and crashed on the floor by the door through which they had entered, shattering into pieces.

223

'Will you be quiet!' snapped Kinga. 'Keep your thoughts to yourself until we are safely out of here.'

At that moment, the giant moved forward, passing between them like a damp cloud brushing a mountaintop.

'Do not touch!' cried the minotaur as the giant raised his hand to the wall. It was too late: Hoo thrust one great finger into the mark. With a rumble and a roar, the wall fell in upon them and they were deluged by a tide of dark water. The flood flowed past them. It swirled around the legs of the child who stood gazing down at it, making no effort to save herself. Kinga clutched on to Morjik to prevent herself being swept away; the minotaur grabbed the end of the dragon's tail as he was buffeted back by the waves. Kira struggled against the tide and was only saved by grabbing hold of Windfoal's horn. Storm-Bird flapped above the flood, clinging on to Eagle-Child's jacket to prevent him from being sucked under. The weather giant scooped Ivor Coddrington out of the water.

'Save the girl!' Kinga shrieked to the weather giant, but Hoo did nothing. Then the child, laughing wildly, lifted her face to the ceiling, threw her arms wide and fell back into the water. The weather giant roared his approval. The other Trustees watched in horror as the girl was swept away, spinning like a leaf borne on a rain-swollen stream.

'We had better get out of here!' bellowed the minotaur. 'Break your bond before it is too late!'

On his command, the creatures abruptly ended

the encounter and returned to consciousness at the entrance to the mine.

Evelyn, Col, and Mack were lying in a heap at the base of the rock wall like discarded toys. Connie had gone.

16

Reaping the Whirlwind

Col was shaken back into consciousness by Eagle-Child. Opening his eyes, he found the side of his head was aching and that there was a trickle of something wet running down his cheek. Groaning as he sat up, he wiped it away and, in the dying light of the fire, discovered that it was blood.

'What happened?' he muttered.

Eagle-Child looked relieved to hear him speak. 'Where are you hurt, Col? Can you move?'

Col waggled his feet experimentally and lifted his arms. Apart from the pain from his head, he was unharmed. 'I'm fine,' he said. Suddenly remembering where he was, he looked around for his father and Evelyn. Kinga and Kira were helping them sit up. Morjik was reviving the fire to cast more light on their injuries. The minotaur galloped past the dragon and up the path out of the dell, disappearing in the darkness. Ivor Coddrington was sitting on a boulder with his head in his hands.

'What happened?' Col asked again. 'Where's Connie?'

'We hoped you three could tell us,' said Eagle-Child, pulling him up and guiding him to a seat nearer the fire. 'We really need to know everything you saw.'

Col dredged back in his memory to the last thing he could remember. He had sat for what seemed like hours with Mack and Evelyn, waiting for the Trustees to return from their trance. It had been weird watching their bodies, all perfectly still with the exception of Connie's. Her face had been screwed up in concentration and Col could read the conflicting stream of emotions passing across it: laughter, anger, fear—and then . . .

'I remember seeing Connie's eyes open all of a sudden,' said Col. 'I thought she had ended the encounter but then I realized she didn't seem to be herself.' The scene was replaying before his mind like a slow-motion film. 'It was like she was asleep or something. Evelyn got up to check she was OK but next thing we knew Connie was all wrapped up in a kind of dark mist—it seemed to be coming from inside her somehow—pouring out of her skin. She began to spin, at first slowly but getting faster and faster. Evelyn tried to grab her arm but Connie pushed her away. It was like Evelyn weighed no more than a doll—she flew through the air and smashed against the rocks. Dad and I also tried to reach Connie and I suppose the same thing happened to us.'

'Yes,' said Eagle-Child. 'You were all thrown against the wall.'

The realization that something dreadful had happened in the encounter hit Col as hard as his earlier collision with the rock face. 'What did you do to her?'

'The weather giant touched the mark. Kullervo broke through,' Eagle-Child replied, his dark eyes smouldering with anger.

Satisfied that Mack was not seriously injured, Kinga came over to Col. 'From what Mack's saying, it appears that Kullervo has only been waiting to seize Connie the moment he was able to break through inside.' She paused, struggling with the burden of responsibility this news thrust on her. She took a deep breath. 'It is time. The moment we all feared has arrived: the universal is under his sway.'

'Summon the Society!' growled Morjik, flexing his wings in preparation for take-off.

'Yes!' said Kira, who was just finishing tying a sling around Evelyn's left arm. 'We'll need everyone who is close enough to help us.'

'Do you have an emergency procedure?' Kinga asked Evelyn urgently.

'Of course,' Evelyn nodded. Her face was white but her jaw was set against the pain of her broken arm. Digging awkwardly inside her jacket she pulled out her phone. Catching on fast, Col got out his own. They had rehearsed this many times before. 'Col, you start with Dr Brock—he's got the cascade list. I'll phone the Mastersons—they're closest.'

Col selected the doctor's number from his directory. In a quiet house in Hescombe a phone was now ringing in the dark, shattering its sleepy peace.

'Yes?' The doctor sounded alert, despite having been awoken.

Kinga took the phone from Col. 'Francis, we've lost Connie to Kullervo. Get everyone to the headland.'

Col heard the tinny voice of the doctor replying: 'I'll set the emergency call-out in progress and come right away.'

The alarm raised, Col wondered what they would do next. Where was Connie now? The wind was mounting. The trees above the dell creaked. Flocks of dead leaves scurried around their feet. There was a sharp crack like a whip, followed by a crash: a tree toppled from the top of the rock face and tumbled into the valley, showering the onlookers with twigs. Something leapt over the fallen trunk: it was the minotaur, charging back to them from his lookout post on the hilltop.

'They are heading towards the white towers,' he bellowed. 'Come!'

'No!' said Kinga, placing a hand on Sentinel's shoulder to prevent him leaving so quickly. 'We must not rush in like this. We need to understand. We need a plan.' She turned to Col. 'Tell us what's happening to Connie. You're the only one who knows.'

Col shook his head. 'If it's anything like what happened to me then she'll be in there somewhere, hiding from him. But her bond with him is so much more powerful than anything I experienced.'

'She saved you with the helm?'

'Yes—but that's a universal's tool. I don't think we can do that for her.'

'But the other times,' Kinga persisted, 'when Connie raised the storms, the bond was broken by an encounter with another?'

Col nodded.

'But you were already bonded with her when Kullervo broke through,' Evelyn said in anguished tones. 'It didn't stop him this time.'

'Does anyone have any better suggestions?' Kinga asked, looking to her fellow Trustees. They shook their heads. 'Then we must try to reach her this way. If one of our creatures can get through, we might be able to save her—and us—before it's too late. If that fails, we'll have to stop her by force. We'll be doing her no favours if we let her live in the power of that evil creature.'

Col choked: it sounded as if they were prepared to sacrifice his friend to stop Kullervo. 'But what about Connie?'

'We have no choice,' said Eagle-Child firmly, standing at Kinga's shoulder. 'The universal would say the same if she were here.'

Evelyn hung her head.

Mack glowered at the Trustees. 'You'd better save her then, or there'll be hell to pay.'

'No more talking,' growled Morjik, a flicker of flame curling from his jaws. 'Let us begin!'

The decision taken, the Trustees followed swiftly on Sentinel's tail. Mack helped Evelyn hobble up the path.

'Here, Coddrington,' he grunted at the companion to weather giants who was lagging behind the others. 'Do something useful for once and give me a hand.'

Without a murmur, Mr Coddrington helped carry Evelyn out of the dell.

When they reached the top of the slope, Col realized how sheltered they had been down there. The wind was blowing so hard that he had difficulty remaining on his feet. Sea-spray flew inland from the waves crashing on the rocks below, stinging Col's eyes. A waning moon hovered on the horizon, dipping in and out from behind fast-moving clouds.

The night was almost over but the storm was only just beginning.

Col took the silver whistle that all companions to pegasi wore on a chain around their necks and blew on it three times. He hoped that the sound would carry to Skylark above the roar of the wind. Without his companion creature, he could do nothing to help. Kinga was already mounting Morjik and preparing to take off. Kira galloped away on the back of Windfoal, the unicorn's mane streaming in the gale. Eagle-Child sprinted after them, Storm-Bird gliding on the winds overhead, the edges of its wings glistening with white light.

'Where's your companion?' Mack asked Mr Coddrington roughly. 'If there was ever a time when we could use a weather giant, it's now.'

'He's gone,' Mr Coddrington gasped. 'I don't know what's become of him, or why he did what he did.'

'Mack,' said Evelyn, slumping against the Trustee. 'Get going. He can help me from here. You're needed at sea. Save Connie for me.'

Mack released his hold on her and gave her a swift kiss. 'Go back to Hugh's. I'll see you there. Come on, Col.'

Leaving Evelyn swaying in Mr Coddrington's arms, father and son ran up to the headland, Mack pulling Col along against the wind. Col felt at times that they were running only to stand still, so strong was the force directed against them. Reaching the crest of the hill, they now had a view across to the wind farm only a field away. Col felt his father's grip increase on his forearm, not this time against the gale but in horrified wonder at the prospect before them. The eight newly completed masts were spinning like children's windmills on a sandcastle, so fast that the vanes were blurred. Winding in and out of the turbines was the thin spiralling funnel of a tornado, blue-black against the dark skies flickering with silver fire. Half-glimpsed at the pinnacle of the pillar of wind, twisting in a pirouette like a demented ballerina was the tiny figure of Connie, arms outstretched, surrendering her body to the force sustaining her.

Col watched as first Morjik and then Storm-Bird threw themselves towards Connie, but each time the wind spun them off, sending them skidding across the skies. Kira and Windfoal had been blown over and were now rolling down the slope towards the cottages. Sentinel and Eagle-Child were both clinging to the same turbine in an attempt to remain on their feet. More Society members were appearing from all sides. Mr Masterson, astride the giant boar with gilded tusks, charged up the hill, closely followed by Rat on Icefen. The twister flicked in their direction, spinning the creatures up into the air and unceremoniously dumping them on a pile of earth left by the builders, their riders half-buried beneath them. Tiles from the cottage roofs showered around them, smashing into thousands of shards. Dr Brock and Argot swooped in from the east only to be knocked back. Argot collided with one of the masts and tumbled to the earth, Dr Brock clinging desperately on by his fingertips. When they hit the ground, neither of them moved.

Col started to sprint towards them, but pulled up, stopped by a familiar presence close at hand. He turned to see Skylark make an ungainly landing some metres away, the white feathers of his wings ruffling the wrong way in the wind, mane and tail whipping furiously. Overhead he heard the swoosh of the chestnut stallion: Firewings, with Captain Graves on his back, going to the rescue of the dragon and his companion. Mack released his son's arm.

'Off you go, Col!' he shouted, pushing him towards Skylark. 'I'm going to find the Kraken.' Mack staggered down the hill, heading for the cove.

Col threw his arms around Skylark's neck and was greeted by a burst of the creature's electrifying presence.

'This is it!' he shouted to his mount. 'I'd hoped this would never happen.'

'But it has, Companion,' said Skylark. 'Let's do what we can for Connie.'

233

The tornado was now spinning away from the wind farm and out to sea, trees bending aside like blades of grass as it passed.

'We must fly high!' Col told Skylark. 'Everyone who's tried to reach her has been thrown off. Let's try dropping down to her.'

Skylark galloped in pursuit of the twister. The funnel of wind teetered on the edge of the cliff for a moment then passed over to hit the surface of the sea, sucking water up like a giant straw. As the pegasus followed, the ground gave way beneath his hooves, leaving him striding for a moment in mid-air. He plummeted downwards. With a quick down-beat of his wings, Skylark regained control. A large chunk of cliff slid down to hit the water, sending a shock wave rippling out to sea, clashing with the incoming rollers with furious energy.

Skylark was still managing to climb, despite being thrown this way and that by the gusting wind. They had reached a height where Col could look down into the funnel. Connie was still spinning, her head flopped forward and hair flying out over her face.

'Connie!' he screamed, quite uselessly as there was no way she would hear him over the roar of the storm. But it seemed that something else heard him: the blue-black spiral elongated, rising to swallow up the horse and rider.

'Evade!' yelled Col.

Skylark dived to the right. The teetering funnel caught him by the back legs and sent him spinning out of control. The world whirled past. Col clung

234

on as they hurtled back to land. The pegasus, with a Herculean effort, managed to slow his tumble. They landed heavily on the sand of the little cove, Col thrown headfirst over his mount's neck. Col put a hand to his head. His vision had become blurred. Rubbing his eyes to clear his sight, he scrambled up on to Skylark's back and looked out to sea. He could see a tiny black figure in the grip of one of the Kraken's tentacles heading out to the twister. The storm itself now seemed to have stopped moving and was gathering in size, swelling as it sucked up more and more water.

'Kullervo's making a tidal wave,' said Skylark. 'We must warn the others.' He began to trot unsteadily up the path, hooves lagging with exhaustion, heading back to the cottages. Lights were blazing and there was a small crowd of people staring dumbstruck in his direction. Too tired to care, Col and Skylark pressed on. Even to Col's numbed brain it was clear what had happened: a storm of this magnitude could not be kept from non-Society members. The mythical creatures had been exposed.

Power. Terror. Strength. Kullervo's companion crowed with triumph as she batted away so easily the creatures trying to attack her. But they were persistent: more and more kept coming to annoy her like mosquitoes whining in her ear and spoiling her beautiful storm.

'Kill them!' said a voice in her head.

Kullervo's companion sent the boy and his horse spinning out of control.

'Why did you not kill them?' asked the voice angrily. 'Are we not here to stamp out our enemies?'

Kullervo's companion laughed wildly. 'I'm not yours to command. You are my companion: I am yours. I don't want to kill them. I want to make the seas leap and the winds do what we will.'

'Then make the elements dance to our tune!' cried Kullervo, twisting her further out to sea. 'Pour my power out upon the waves, draw them up to you and send them onto the land.'

The girl cupped her hands like a potter moulding clay, forming the water into an immense vessel to contain Kullervo's hatred of the human world. It rose up around them, glittering with red-stained foam in the light of the rising sun.

'Good! Good!' he cried. 'And this is only the beginning. See the pleasure we can give each other in our companionship! We can remould the earth as we wish.'

Suddenly, a black tentacle snaked up through the eye of the storm and seized Connie by the waist. It ripped her from the wind's embrace.

'No!' shrieked Kullervo.

The Kraken pulled Connie down the tunnel of wind and plunged her into the sea. The connection broken, the tornado spun out of control, shedding the water it had gathered in a drenching spray.

'Where is my companion?' roared Kullervo.

Connie woke with a start as she hit the water, taking a choking mouthful as she was dragged under. Where was she? Struggling against the creature holding her down, she made panicked kicks to get free. It released her and she broke the surface, gasping

236

for air, only to find the storm-tossed waves dousing her in more water.

'Help!' she screamed.

Someone dived into the water by her side and emerged quickly to take her arm.

'Connie—don't panic: you'll be all right!' said Mack. He kicked towards the shore, fighting the waves.

But things were not going to be all right: out of the sky above them a dark ribbon of wind unfurled from the twister. Connie screamed with terror as she was scooped from the waves and enveloped once more in Kullervo's storm. With no time to raise her shield, Kullervo reclaimed his hold on her, reconnecting with the part of her that was his companion, driving Connie back into unconsciousness.

'We shall never be parted!' Kullervo told her. 'Those that try to come between us shall be punished.' He let drop the remaining waters they had gathered onto the sea, seeking to crush the Kraken and its audacious companion. The weight of water drove the creature deep, Mack clutched in one tentacle. 'Ha!' Kullervo gloated. 'They will not come back for more.'

'No, Companion,' said the girl, her brief rebellion against his presence snuffed out. She smiled. 'Now, where were we?'

17

Exposure

Col slid wearily off Skylark's back and ran into the now roofless cottage. Hugh Lionheart's kitchen had been turned into an emergency room, filled with injured people and the smaller creatures. Hugh was presiding over the arrangements, looking dazed by what the storm had done to his house and the influx of mythical beings but still managing to deal competently with the obvious needs before him. Eagle-Child came in carrying a wood sprite with a shattered leg. Col quickly told him about the tidal wave.

Eagle-Child nodded. 'Come: the Trustees are meeting next door to regroup. Let us bring them your news.'

In the Ratcliff kitchen, Col found many more casualties requiring attention. Mrs Ratcliff, uncharacteristically quelled, as even she could find nothing to say in the face of the extraordinary scene before her, was tending a nasty cut on Mr Masterson's forehead. Mr Ratcliff had taken refuge in a bottle of whisky. He was slumped in a corner, arms around the Alsatian, singing to himself. By the fireplace, Captain Graves was bandaging Dr Brock's wrist. Many other Society members were gathered around the table in fierce debate. Noticing the new arrivals, Gard stamped over to Col and thumped him on the back.

'That was a brave attempt, Col,' he said.

'Yeah, pretty cool,' added Rat. 'Shame it didn't work.'

'No, Kinga!' The room fell silent as Evelyn's voice rang out. 'Not yet! She might still escape! Don't send in the dragons, please!'

Kinga, standing beside Evelyn at the sink, put her head in her hands briefly, but then looked up, her expression resolute.

'What choice do we have? We can't stop Kullervo. Connie is the only weak point. Either we take her out by force and save humanity from annihilation, or leave her with him and we all die, Connie included. The dragons will try to save her—if they can.'

Rat gave a sharp intake of breath.

'But what evidence do we have that she's allowing him to put his plans into action?' protested Evelyn. 'So far no one's been badly injured. She's only been playing with us.'

'I think the playing is about to end,' said Eagle-Child moving forward. 'Col has just told me that Kullervo and the universal are creating a tidal wave.'

Col felt absolutely gutted—with his news he had unwittingly signed Connie's death warrant! It couldn't be!

Kinga turned back to Evelyn. 'Do you need any more convincing? Connie would not wish you to allow this to happen in her name, would she?'

Evelyn shook her head.

'But you can't do this!' Rat cried. 'There must be another way!'

At that moment, the door to the kitchen banged open and Mack staggered in, dripping wet.

'I spoke to her!' he spluttered, interrupted by a fit of coughing. He recovered himself. 'We got her out briefly: she's still there. If only we could reach her for a few more seconds—give her a chance to defend herself.'

'You've got to listen to him!' said Col, hands clenched by his side, determined to fight Connie's corner for her. 'We've got to work as a team to give Connie her few seconds.'

Gard banged his mallet on the table, shattering the crockery. 'They're right. I am not prepared to give up on the universal yet. We must risk one more attempt.'

'I think we need to go back into her mind,' said Col desperately, 'but not just one of us: we need to overwhelm his presence with ours.'

Kinga's eyes lit up with this suggestion. 'Yes!' she said. 'We left her mind so quickly, she had no time to end the encounter—the door is probably still open.'

'What are we waiting for!' said Mr Masterson, pushing Mrs Ratcliff's hand aside and pulling himself up. 'Let's get as near as we can and make a final attempt.'

'Everyone to the beach!' cried Kinga.

There was a mass exodus from the kitchen. Col whistled to Skylark and leapt on his back; Rat vaulted onto Icefen. Soon all the creatures still able to move were pouring down to the beach—boar and frost wolf, dragon and pegasus, selkie and Storm-Bird, unicorn, rock dwarf and many more.

Out on the horizon, the storm had swollen to a gross size. The thin funnel was now a huge inverted cone the size of the Great Pyramid. It weaved drunkenly, bloated with water, waiting to discharge its burden to sweep away the creatures that stood in its way. Col could no longer see Connie: the twister had completely swallowed her.

'Your dad said she's out there?' Rat shook his head in disbelief.

Kinga stood on the top of the wooden steps with Sentinel by her side and held up her hand for silence.

'On my signal, all creatures are to reach out through their bond to the universal. If she hears us and lets us in, follow the minotaur!' She turned to where Dr Brock, Argot, and the other dragon riders were gathered, and said in a lower voice, 'If this fails, stand ready to follow Morjik and me to do what is necessary.' Kinga raised her arm, held them for a second with her stern gaze and then dropped her hand. 'Now!' she commanded.

Col could sense Skylark galloping in his bond towards Connie's presence. He could feel her ahead—a white mist in the darkness, indistinct but definitely there. As they got closer, he became aware of the other creatures: dragons swooped down from above, selkies swam beside him, Icefen loped

241

past, the shadow-Rat clinging to its back. The mist resolved itself into the portal Col had once entered through. Sentinel was already waiting for them as more and more creatures crowded up.

'The way is still open!' Sentinel cried. 'Follow me!'

The minotaur plunged inside Connie's mind. Col, following close behind, was astounded to find that the dark corridors he had visited last time had disappeared. All they could see now was a vast stretch of black water that lapped hungrily around their ankles, sticking to them like oil.

As soon as the minotaur's hooves touched the water, Kullervo was alerted to his presence.

'Who is this trespasser?' He sent a wave of malice to crush the creature that dared encroach on his bond with his companion. The minotaur was washed away, sent reeling back out of the portal. But then Kullervo became aware of more, and yet still more creatures creeping into the universal's mind. None of them individually strong enough to defeat him, but there were so many of them he did not know where to start. Distracted, like a bear driving off a swarm of bees from his honey, Kullervo tried to eject the myriad attacks from rock dwarf and water sprite, banshee and boar with wave after wave. He roared. Dark waters swatted the crowds. Rat could see that Kullervo was holding the breach against them.

'We need to give our friends a chance,' he told Icefen.

The frost wolf nodded, at one with his companion's daring thought.

242

Together, wolf and boy let out an exultant howl, defying Kullervo.

'She's our pack leader,' shouted Rat. 'Give her back!'

As Rat anticipated, Kullervo rose to the challenge to his authority, sending a wave to wash the impudent wolf and boy away. But instead of fleeing the attack, Icefen sprang upon the wave, unleashing his breath. The water crackled, turning to ice for a few precious seconds of forgetfulness before the full might of Kullervo reasserted itself. The frost shattered and the wave expelled Rat and Icefen from Connie's mind.

Those seconds were enough, however, for Col and Skylark to fly past unnoticed. They took refuge in the shadows with Dr Brock and Argot, who had also managed to get across the threshold. Waiting for Kullervo to be preoccupied by a concerted assault from the selkies, pegasus and dragon slipped past Kullervo's vigilance and flew over the waters, hunting for any sign of Connie. At first all seemed black—an endless ocean with no life other than Kullervo's. Then they glimpsed a small white figure, lying on the last patch of dry land still above the waves, like a castaway washed up on a desert island. They flew down to hover above her, stirring her hair with the downdraught of their wings.

'Connie!' Col shouted.

With an effort, the shadow-Connie raised her head from her arms.

'Connie! You must drive him out!'

'I can't,' she said wearily, pulling herself to her knees, hands now over her ears, head shaking from

243

side to side to rid herself of a pain that refused to go away. 'I can't hear myself any more.'

'You must! Grab your shield—helm—anything!' called down Dr Brock. 'We're here to help you, but we need you to help us.'

She opened her eyes and stared at the water surrounding her. 'But look at me! There's nothing left. It's all him—and her—his companion.'

'That's not true,' Col said desperately. 'We can see you. You're still here. Don't let him win.'

Connie moaned in pain.

'The hauberk!' growled the shadow-Argot.

'Yes!' said Dr Brock, his eyes alight with new hope. 'Argot's right. Put on the hauberk. You said it gave you the protective powers of the creature you're bonded with. Let us protect you.'

'I'm so tired,' Connie sobbed. 'Just let me be.'

'No!' Col slid off Skylark's back and dropped down beside her. He pulled her up so that she could slump against him. 'Make this last effort for us—for your friends!'

Connie closed her eyes again, leaning on him. 'I'll try,' she whispered. Slowly, as if weighed down with lead, she raised her hands in the air and plucked an invisible garment from in front of her, pulling it down on her head. As she did so, the hauberk took physical shape before Col's eyes—at first a faint mist that faded out of sight, then reappearing more clearly in the form of a silver mesh stretching to Skylark and Argot.

'Come, join us!' growled Argot to the other mythical creatures.

As more beasts and beings hurried to attach themselves to the hauberk, the links wrapped themselves around Col and Connie. Col felt his excitement building.

'Get up, Connie,' he said, pushing her to her feet. 'Drive him out!'

'I can't. Just let me sit here,' she said, closing her eyes.

'No,' Col said fiercely. This was no time to give in to his pity for her suffering. He shook her awake. 'You are the most powerful being in the Society. You're his match. I can't believe that the Connie I know would just let him take her over without a struggle. We're all with you.'

Calling on the last embers of her strength, Connie stood up unsteadily and took a step off her island. The water parted at her feet, leaving bare rock floor. Gaining in strength, she swept her arms wide, forcing the waters back so she could walk dry-footed across the floor of her own mind. With each step, she claimed more and more space for herself.

Kullervo, realizing that resistance to his presence was building within, turned from the creatures he had been trying to expel. He bore down on Connie in the form of a curling wave. But Connie was no longer alone. On the flick of her wrist, silver dragon fire scorched the surge, turning the crest of the wave to steam. Still it came. She bent her head. A corner of the hauberk lifted up and began to spin like dancing banshees. The twisting chain collided with the breaker, dispersing some of its force.

'You are mine!' cried Kullervo in fury.

'But I'm theirs too!' Connie shouted defiantly.

Punching her fist in the air, part of the mail unlinked itself from the rest and curled into the shape of a giant boar. It charged at Kullervo's wave and smashed against it, blocking its path with its formidable bulk so that the water washed against it and fell back. Then Connie pointed to the ground and the mail struck down like a rock dwarf's mallet. It split the rock floor, opening up a deep fissure. Kullervo's flood tumbled over the edge, disappearing from view. As the last trickle of water was sucked away, she made a final effort to seal the fissure shut with another swipe of her mallet—and fell forward onto the dry ground.

At that moment, Col was catapulted from the universal's mind and crashed back to consciousness in his own body. All around him, creatures and people were groaning from their rude eviction.

'Did we do enough?' Col asked anyone who could hear him.

'You did something, that's for sure,' said Rat as he helped Col to his feet. 'The twister's spun itself out. It vanished a moment ago.'

'Connie!' cried Evelyn, throwing off Ivor Coddrington's arm and rushing to the sea.

Without her having to say another word, Col leapt on Skylark; Mack and Arran ran down the beach and dived into the water. The dragon and pegasus riders scrambled onto their mounts and took off. Col and Skylark were almost the first on the scene. Another creature had been there all the time. Connie was lying on her back in the water, eyes closed, supported above the waves by a tentacle of the Kraken. The seal-head of the selkie bobbed out of the water moments later. Grabbing Connie's jacket in his teeth, Arran began to tow her back to shore, soon joined by Mack. Flying in a majestic circle, the dragons and pegasi turned for land.

A few metres from the shore, Arran rippled back into his human body and helped Mack carry Connie up the beach. A crowd of people rushed forward to lift the unconscious girl out of the water.

'Lay her on her side,' commanded Evelyn. 'Give her room.'

Coughing, Connie opened her eyes and rolled onto her back, staring up at the clear sky fringed with familiar faces. She smiled slightly.

'Thanks,' she whispered.

Col helped her to sit up. Connie's eyes fell on Icefen, sitting on his haunches behind Rat, tongue panting eagerly. 'I s'pose I'm going to have to ask you to clear up my mess for me,' she said wistfully. It seemed so unfair now that her uncle and the others would suffer because of her.

'We thought you'd never ask!' said Rat with a grin. With an excited howl from the wolf, Rat leapt onto Icefen's back and set off for the cottages.

'Don't worry, Connie,' said Dr Brock quietly as he helped her to her feet. 'When they wake up, they'll remember very little.'

Back at the cottages, Connie saw that Rat had begun with his own family. His mother was lying sprawled on the doorstep, a rolling pin still clasped in her hand. Uncle Hugh sat propped up against her, mouth open, snoring loudly.

Kinga turned to Connie. 'We will clear this up,' she told her, hugging her tightly to her chest. 'You go and get some rest. We'll talk about what happened when you've had a chance to recover.'

Connie nodded wearily. She was now beyond the point where she could do anything more for herself.

Hugh's cottage had been rendered uninhabitable by the storm, the ceiling of her bedroom open to the sky, so Mack drove her and Evelyn back to Shaker Row in her aunt's Citroën. With her good arm, Evelyn helped Connie change out of her wet clothes and smoothed down her covers after she had fallen into her bed.

'Sleep now, Connie,' she said, opening the window to let in Argand. The little dragon curled up on Connie's feet. Evelyn shut the door as she left. As Connie closed her eyes, she heard again the hiss of the black waters lapping in the depths, but then the glowing presence of the dragon burnt the darkness away, leaving only a sense of warmth and peace. She slept.

18
Healing

'It's good to see you up and around again!' said Hugh as Connie came down for breakfast on Monday morning. He was a refugee at Shaker Row while the builders repaired the damage to his home.

Outside, Connie could see two bemused council workers in the back garden, rolling up tape and shaking their heads over the curiously sound cliff. They had rushed round after the storm, expecting to find the slope had weakened still further, but instead discovered a phenomenon previously unknown to geological science: the storm had somehow mended the faults.

'Are you sure you're quite over your flu?' asked Hugh.

'Yes, thanks,' said Connie as she packed her school bag. 'All I needed was a couple of days in bed.'

He handed her a mug of tea and looked into her face with concern. 'Yes, you look well enough for school. A bit pale perhaps, but nothing serious.' He ruffled her hair. 'Ouch!' Sparks had leapt from it and stung his fingers. 'I keep forgetting about that strange mop of yours.'

She smoothed her hair down: it had become particularly lively after the multiple encounters of Saturday morning and still tingled with energy. In fact, every part of her being seemed to crackle with residual power as though her internal batteries had been overcharged.

'It was kind of you to stop me coming in and catching your bug,' Hugh said, settling back in his chair. 'I wouldn't've minded nursing you, of course, but Evelyn said she could manage and, to tell you the truth, I've been feeling a bit odd myself since Saturday.'

'Oh yes?' asked Connie carefully, setting her mug down.

Hugh looked out of the window, deep in thought. 'Yes, I caught a chill and it brought on some very strange dreams. Must've been the storm. Maybe I took a blow to the head—not surprising with so much stuff flying about.'

'What kind of dreams, Uncle Hugh?'

'Funny ones, now I come to think of it. I dreamt that you'd become a spinning top and I couldn't catch you.'

'Oh?' Connie tried to keep her voice level. 'That is strange.'

Hugh looked down at the tablets he took for his heart condition, ranged on the breakfast table in front of him. 'Or maybe it's the new pills the doctor gave me, because the dream got stranger and stranger—full of flying horses, and dragons, if you believe me!'

'Oh, I believe you.'

'I haven't dreamt of dragons since I was a child,' he mused. 'And then there was Rat riding on some big dog—as if Wolf had grown overnight into a monster. Funny how the mind plays out your fears about things, isn't it?' He looked up at Connie enquiringly.

'Yes, very funny.'

'Well, you'd better get ready. I'll drop you at school.'

'I'll just look in on Evelyn first,' said Connie, buttering herself a sandwich to take in the car. 'I think she's still in bed.'

'Good idea. Very unfortunate that she broke her arm. Blown over by the storm, no less. Whatever next?'

'I don't know, Uncle Hugh,' said Connie. 'I really don't know.'

A full day at school tired Connie out and she was looking forward to getting home. Col walked her to her door, carrying her bag for her.

'Are you sure you're OK, Connie?' he asked. 'I'm surprised your head's stopped spinning after what you went through.'

'I'm fine. I feel all used up but otherwise fine. To be honest, I prefer being at school with you all to sitting thinking about it at home.' She sighed. 'Sometimes, Col, I wish I was ordinary.'

'Nah, you don't. Think what you'd miss out on!'

'Yeah, possession by Kullervo; almost wiping out the human race; having my mind a battleground— what a shame that would be.'

Col looked at her sideways, trying to work out what she really felt under the irony. 'Are you OK about us all invading you like we did? If it was me, I'd hate to have loads of people trampling all over my mind.'

Connie shrugged. 'Of course, I don't like being invaded. But I'm really grateful that you did what you did. And d'you know something?' She looked up at him. Her eyes were shining.

'No, what?'

'Though it's been a rough ride for me in the Society lately, I was really touched by the way everyone in the end worked together to save me. That's a very good memory—it helps.'

'I'm glad,' he said, wishing he was more eloquent and could put into words all that he had thought and felt about the events of Saturday.

They had reached her gate.

'And I won't forget what you did for me—the way you refused to let me give up,' she said.

'Course I wouldn't let you. What are friends for?'

As he handed over her school bag, she leant forward and quickly kissed him on the cheek.

'Thanks, Col. You're one in a million,' she whispered in his ear. She went inside quickly before he had a chance to reply, leaving him rubbing his face thoughtfully.

'Mind your step!' called Sentinel back down the line of creatures and people following him into the mines. 'There is a shaft on your left.'

Light from torches rippled over the walls and spilled onto the floor. Only a metre from Connie's feet yawned a black pit. A frayed rope dangled down into it from a winch suspended over the hole like a forgotten fisherman sitting at his rod. She did not like to ask herself what he might catch one day from the lightless depths of the mine.

'Where are you taking us, Sentinel?' she asked as she edged cautiously round the pit, her hand clasped in his.

'To my chamber. But we must go the long way round so that the larger creatures can reach it.'

Behind her Connie heard the thump of Morjik leaping over the shaft, closely followed by the muffled clip-clop of Windfoal and Skylark. Morjik's ruff of scales scraped on the uneven ceiling: he had to slither along on his belly to get through the passageways.

'I hope it's not much further,' Col whispered to Connie on her other side. 'If your bodyguard carries on like this, I'm not sure there'll be much left of the dragons by the time we've squeezed our way in.'

'Almost there, Companion to Pegasi,' boomed Sentinel.

Col could have kicked himself for forgetting about the acute hearing of the minotaur.

Sentinel turned a final corner and put his shoulder against a pair of wooden doors with rusted hinges. They creaked slowly open, grating on the floor, revealing the minotaur's sparkling chamber lit with a roaring fire. Smoke curled up to the ceiling and out through a hidden channel to the surface to where the wind turbines were slowly revolving in the light breeze. All of the mine-dwellers were gathered, waiting for their guests.

Connie, Col, the Trustees and the members of the Chartmouth Chapter of the Society filed in. For many it was the first time in the mine and they stared around at the maimed creatures, uncertain of what they should do, looking to someone to lead them. Mrs Clamworthy, bringing up the rear on Gard's arm, clucked her tongue irritably.

'Well, sit down in your places, all of you,' she said, ushering Jessica Moss and Shirley Masterson forward. Gard helped her over to the water sprites positioned at the northerly point of the chamber and she placed herself amongst them, greeting them with the low murmuring song of her companion species. The other members rapidly got the right idea and split off into their respective companies, leaving Connie, Col, Rat, Sentinel, and the Trustees standing in the centre of the room.

'OK, Connie?' said Col.

'Yes, this time,' she smiled back. 'You go and sit down.'

'Okey-dokey,' said Rat and he pulled Col after him to take their places.

Kinga put her arm around Connie's shoulders and held up her hand for silence.

'Friends,' she began, looking up at the minotaur, 'welcome all, especially to those who have been estranged from the Society for too long. We are here this evening to set the record straight. We have an apology to make to our universal. The

Society has not treated her well over the last few months, failing to nurture her gift and help her in her need. However, the Trustees also recognize that not all of us were guilty in this respect— Connie is blessed with many loyal friends—and you risked much to go against the Society's rules. Thank you.'

A murmur went round the chamber. Captain Graves shook his head doubtfully.

'Firstly, I wish you all to know that the investigation by the Trustee responsible for the Company of the Elementals has revealed the truth of what happened in the two most recent storms. My colleague will take up the story for me from here.'

Kinga nodded to Mr Coddrington. He stepped forward, his shoulders hunched, head down, and pulled out a file from his briefcase. Connie wondered what was coming: she could not imagine Mr Coddrington ever saying anything to her advantage.

'My investigation . . . ' Mr Coddrington was barely audible.

'Speak up!' bellowed Erik Ulvsen from among the Elementals.

Mr Coddrington cleared his throat awkwardly. 'My investigation has shown that the snowstorm in early January was caused by a weather giant. The same weather giant was responsible for a serious breach of the universal's defences last Friday night with the grave consequences we all witnessed. The universal is cleared of any blame for either incident. The weather giant has been suspended from the Society until such time as it can be established whether he was acting alone or on the orders of Kullervo. Unfortunately, he has not been available for questioning.'

'Come on, man,' shouted Mack from the Sea Snakes, 'it's clear the creature's a traitor. Why else would he create the snowstorm? Someone must've put him up to it.'

Mr Coddrington was silent, shuffling his papers and pretending he had not heard the intervention. Col glanced over at Connie: she was gazing at the Trustee, biting her bottom lip. He could tell that she knew something and he thought he could guess what it was.

'Perhaps Mr Coddrington might like to tell us what he was doing on the night of the snowstorm?' Col called out. Connie flicked her gaze over to him. He knew from her expression that he had guessed correctly. 'I think Connie's already said that Kullervo was not present at the time. Someone else who knew that the other Trustees were arriving may've wanted her to look bad before her appeal.'

An angry muttering broke out in the chamber.

'Shame on you, Coddrington!' Mr Masterson said loudly from the back rows of the Two-Fours.

Mr Coddrington still did not look up but his fingers were now frozen on the page he was holding. He coughed.

'In view of the suspension of my former companion, Hoo, I will naturally be relinquishing my post as Trustee. New elections will be held in due course.' He looked to Kinga. 'Is that all?'

Kinga nodded. 'You can go.'

Dismissed, Mr Coddrington slunk away to the back rows of the Elementals. The greeting he received there was far from ecstatic and he was left sitting on his own with a large gap between him and his nearest neighbour. Icefen sneezed in his direction, coating his jacket in frosty droplets.

'Would the universal like to say anything?' Kinga asked.

Connie nodded. 'I'd just like to thank everyone for risking so much to help me on Friday night. I know not all of you even liked me—'

'It's not a question of liking!' broke in Captain Graves. 'We like you well enough. We were just damned scared of you!' Many heads nodded. 'You were always so mysterious.'

Connie looked down at her hands, twisting them nervously together. Col feared for a moment that she had lost the courage to speak out but then she raised her head and looked directly at Captain Graves.

'If you want the truth, Captain, I'm more afraid of myself than any of you can possibly be. But what do you expect me to do about it? I am what I am and I have to live with that—good and bad. I s'pose you'd better learn to live with it too.'

Erik startled everyone by suddenly letting out a howl of delight as his pack leader asserted her position as top dog. Rat, Icefen, and the great wolves joined in so that the cave resounded with their cries. Captain Graves's chin was up, his eyes glittering, but Col could tell from the amused curve of his lips that his mentor was impressed by the universal's spirit.

Connie held up her hand for silence. The howls faded.

'And as for being mysterious, I think I've been the most open of us recently. After all, you've been trampling across my mind—you can hardly say you don't know me now.'

'I think,' said Dr Brock rising to his feet, 'that it's about time the Chartmouth Chapter—and the Society at large, of course—accepts that we are not just here for Elementals and Sea Snakes, High Flyers and Two-Fours, we are also here for the company of the universals. It's a small, select company admittedly,' (his eyes twinkled at Connie) 'but one with as much right to be here as any of us.' He directed a significant look at Ivor Coddrington. 'This may, of course, involve a few painful changes to our way of doing things—we might, for example, have to think of a new way to mentor our trainee universal, as clearly there is no one-to-one option here—but we must embrace these changes and not blame the universal for challenging our old habits.'

'The Trustees entirely agree with you, Francis,' said Kinga. 'As a practical expression of this, Gard has volunteered to be Connie's chief mentor responsible for her progress. Are you happy with this, Connie?'

Connie nodded. She looked over to where Gard was sitting beside the rock dwarf with the cracked head. He raised his mallet in salute.

'And our friend Sentinel has volunteered to organize full-time protection for the universal to prevent any further attacks by Kullervo from inside or out. Are you content with this, Connie?'

'Of course,' she said, smiling up at the minotaur.

'Then that is all we have to say for now,' said Kinga, moving to signal the conclusion of the meeting.

'No, it's not all,' said Connie quickly, gesturing around the room. 'What about our friends here who need healing?'

Kinga paused, her face in doubt. 'We want to help, but what can we do for them?'

The minotaur grunted. 'I have told you, Trustee. It is she who can help us, not you.'

'No, you're wrong, Sentinel,' said Connie. 'I now finally understand what I must do. It was Friday night that taught me this. The universal has no power of her own. I can only channel or borrow yours. With my help, you can heal each other. You just have to work as one—as a pack, dare I say.' She smiled at the wolves.

'But can you do this?' asked Kinga cautiously. 'Can you sustain so many bonds at one time? You did something similar once, I know, for Morjik but there were only four creatures in that bond.'

'I did it on Friday night to save myself; surely I can do it today to save others?' Connie sat down at Sentinel's feet. She felt a new confidence, a right to tell them what to do as she knew instinctively it would work. 'Join with me, please. We are going to use the sword.'

After a brief flurry of activity as creatures and people settled themselves for concentration, the room fell silent. In Connie's mind, however, there was a rush of wings and a stampede of feet as beasts and beings approached from all sides. Throwing out silvery ribbon-like links to each, Connie stood at the centre of a wheel, its glistening spokes revolving slowly around her. With a sweeping gesture of her hand, the ribbons began to twist around each other, like the strips of metal forged together by a blacksmith into a sprung-steel sword. Each took strength from the other. The sword set to work. Water sprites filtered through the rocky layers of the dwarves emerging pristine and sparkling. Wood sprites received the nurturing touch of water, sprouting new limbs and healing wounds in their bark. The power of roots crumbled the edges of cracks in the stone and carved new beautiful faces for the rock dwarves. Winged beasts found forgetfulness for past hurts in the frost wolf's breath. Each creature found another with the gift to meet its need; all were able to help in the healing.

The task complete, with a deft twist of her arm the sword unravelled, each connection unfurling back to single ribbons, stretching to Connie like strings on a maypole. Casting these into the air, Connie ended the encounter, allowing the links to flutter gently to the ground.

There was complete silence in the chamber. Connie sat slumped forward, head bowed in exhaustion.

'You did it!' exclaimed Sentinel. 'You healed us!'

Connie sat up, shaking her hair back. 'No, we did it. You all healed each other.'

This distinction was lost on the jubilant creatures who now poured out of their places at the edge of the circle and crowded around Connie, touching her hand, stroking her hair, showing off their restored bodies to her. The minotaur had to lift her onto his shoulder to prevent her being swamped by an over-enthusiastic group of water sprites.

Connie looked down into his face and saw that his eye was still clouded.

'But your eye,' she said, disappointed, 'that's not healed?'

The minotaur shook his head. 'No, but I am. I was healed the moment you gave me back my name. What is one blind eye? I am whole and proud to be your Sentinel.'

Over amongst the Two-Fours, Col sensed that the bond had brought healing too to Skylark's bruised feelings about the wind farm. It was time to move on. So Col was delighted to see his companion spontaneously trot over to Icefen and stand at his shoulder in a gesture of friendship. Rat fondled the pegasus's nose and made the introduction. Col was about to join them when Captain Graves tapped him on the back. He turned reluctantly from the scenes of celebration to his mentor.

'That's one fine girl over there, my boy,' Captain Graves said, nodding at Connie. 'I hope you didn't listen to me and go and jilt her?'

'I didn't,' Col said with a grin at Rat. 'I'm not that stupid.'

Julia Golding is a multi-award winning writer for
young people. A former British diplomat and Oxfam
policy adviser, she has now published over fifty
books in genres ranging from historical adventure
to fantasy. Read carefully and you'll spot all sorts
of material from her diplomatic and Oxfam careers
popping up in unexpected places. She has a doctorate
in English literature from Oxford.

Have you read them all?

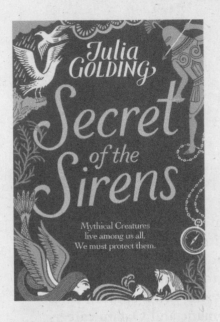

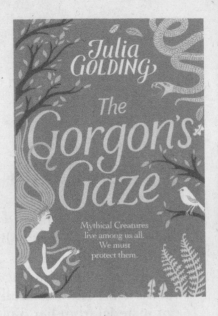

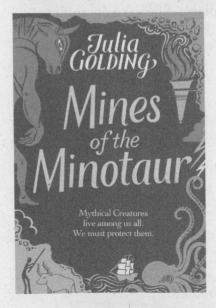